DATE DUE

BA 2013	
N.E.B.-10-16-13	
BA	

PRINTED IN U.S.A.

BURN ENGLISH

Center Point
Large Print

This Large Print Book carries the
Seal of Approval of N.A.V.H.

BURN ENGLISH

WILLIAM A. LUCKEY

CENTER POINT LARGE PRINT
THORNDIKE, MAINE

This Center Point Large Print edition
is published in the year 2013 by arrangement with
Golden West Literary Agency.

The text of this Large Print edition is unabridged.
In other aspects, this book may vary
from the original edition.
Printed in the United States of America
on permanent paper.
Set in 16-point Times New Roman type.

ISBN: 978-1-61173-779-0

Library of Congress Cataloging-in-Publication Data

Luckey, William A.
Burn English / William A. Luckey.
pages ; cm.
ISBN 978-1-61173-779-0 (library binding : alk. paper)
1. Wild horses—Fiction. 2. Horse breeders—Fiction.
   3. Large type books. I. Title.
PS3612.U265B87 2013
813′.6—dc23
                                                              2012051788

For Margaret MacGregor Full Perry Luckey
1903—2007

PROLOGUE

The sound was clear and strong, moving with him, underneath him. A horse in full gallop, Burn lying close to the sweaty neck, urging on the horse with hands and voice, asking for longer strides—faster, even faster. The dark colt responded with a leap that almost unseated Burn, and he grabbed the black mane, fought for air.

Then it was the gray horse laboring and exhausted short-strided. Time to quit. But there were other horses in a green clearing . . . horses dying . . . bloody . . . tangled. He had to save them.

He woke from the dream, the familiar panic slow to leave, the taste of old copper in his mouth. He spat to one side, saw the reddish stain, knew he'd bitten the inside of his mouth, or had been coughing, that deep cough bent on destroying him.

The dark colt was now an aging, lamed stallion way past his prime; the gray had died twenty years ago—a rogue outlaw that had given everything he had had to Burn, but it hadn't been enough. Burn couldn't save the horses then, couldn't save himself, either.

He shook his hands, warily stood from the

narrow bed, and forced himself outside to the shaded sun, the valley spread out in full view of the cabin. Then he understood why he'd dreamed his repeated dream in midday. Hoof beats of a horse pulling a buggy.

The driver waved. Burn barely raised his hand. Davey Hildahl, off on an errand to Springerville, cattle sales or new breeding stock or some fool chore the ranch owner thought only the foreman could handle.

After a quick breakfast, he would make a ride to the Hildahl homestead, knowing Davey was gone for two days. He saddled the bay mare, slowly smoothing out the blanket, setting the gear straight and balanced on her back, doing up the *cincha* real easy. She wasn't skittish or spoiled, but she was sensitive, thin-skinned, and Burn was always careful with this particular mare. In his mind she was the best of the lot, much like her daddy but with a lady's sweetness of temper and generosity that made her satisfying simply to look at from a horseman's point of view. Riding her was his only true pleasure.

It took him an easy hour's ride to the Meiklejon Ranch headquarters. The older folks in the area, they still called it the Littlefield spread, the owner that Meiklejon had bought the land from, the man who'd carved out a ranch against Indians and wild animals. Littlefield had died quickly after selling out. Burn had heard that the payments went to some relative back East. Some niece, a sister's child.

The Littlefield place appeared on a rise, now the grand home of Gordon Meiklejon, its stone front shadowed by a wide ramada, or verandah as the gentleman himself called it. Burn had been inside only once because there had been a longstanding coolness between him and Meiklejon. A distrust of the other born of a harsh accident, an understanding about what Meiklejon's decision to put up wire had cost Burn. They nodded politely to each other when meeting for celebrations at the Hildahl place. That was room enough for each man, and the distance they kept from one another was honored by those who surrounded them.

She would be in the kitchen, so he put up the mare in an empty side corral, then stood on the bottom step to the back door of the old house. He remembered his trip here that one summer when his blood had soaked into the railing, the top step, even on the doorframe itself. Twenty years of weather and scrubbing had not erased that awful time.

When he knocked, she laughed and told him to come in, that he wasn't a formal visitor. He belonged here, she said. The words stunned him, as they did each time she spoke them. He had learned she did not understand his feelings, would not allow herself to remember how it felt when she had washed his body, fed him, tended to him that summer. The bond such intimacy created had not gone from him even when she had made her choice, and the choice had been Davey.

Katherine Donald Hildahl might be twenty years older now, but she was still beautiful to Burn—tall and straight, her brown hair now lightened by strands of gray, and her eyes fine and watchful. Laughter showed at her mouth, and in those eyes there was an ease and pleasure as he presented himself to her, offering his hand, which she took and used to pull him closer, to give him that soft kiss on the cheek. To her it was a gesture; to him it was agony.

She had carried five children, one of them dying at birth, and still she was slender and graceful, and each move, as she worked at her chores, drew him closer inside the kitchen walls. It was a familiar room, safe, a place he'd once wanted for himself.

"You look sorrowful, Burn. Anything Davey and I can do?"

There it was—the cause of his sorrow. She didn't realize the pain caused by her own words. He forced a grin, knowing it would look terrible, but he wasn't given to easy smiles and careless chatter. He took a chair from the worn table, pulled it to where he could sit and watch her, lean on the back of the chair, and say nothing. She would eventually smile at him absently, as if barely acknowledging him as her hands shaped a loaf of bread or fashioned a pie crust.

Burn English was his usual self, quiet and too thoughtful, holding doggedly to his out-dated way of life. A quality Katherine had once admired in him, she now knew it was no longer useful, not when the world around them was changing so quickly. Not when his reliance on himself and the horses he bred and raised were no longer productive. This single-minded determination would destroy him. Not like the barbed wire had those years past, when the destruction had been physical, a bleeding death he barely escaped.

Time had brought about changes having to do with motion and possibilities—telephones that let you speak to distant neighbors without the effort of a buggy trip, motorcars that terrified the horses and delighted the men and children. Burn saw none of these changes, refused to see, and for that Katherine mourned him.

She knew that he loved her still, had never stopped loving her. But the decision had come from her heart when she had waited in this very kitchen years ago, standing between Burn and Davey, steadied by their physical presence as she had learned of her father's death. It was Davey she had turned to, instinct telling her this was the man who could offer protection and comfort.

Burn's face, as she had moved from him to Davey, had been one of the most terrible things she had ever witnessed. That pain going deeper than any bullet or cutting wire, a pain to the soul, impossible to heal. All these years and he had never pressed her, always had held back from that small kiss she gave him each visit. She needed that contact, the smell of him, that breathing in his heart, reminding her that she had made the right choice. Davey could be difficult; any man worth his salt was hard-headed and determined. But Davey cared for the children he had given her, and, when she studied Burn, she could not see him as a father. All these years and Katherine still wished for Burn the pleasure and contentment she had created with Davey.

Looking straight at Burn now, she saw his head tilt, the black hair filled with gray, the green eyes tight at the corners, the harsh face drawn with wrinkles but no loose flesh on his body, no small belly like her Davey carried. There was no one to care for Burn and make certain he was eating well, to wash his clothes, and to keep his bed. Only loneliness—and the horses for company.

She turned, smiling. "Here, Burn. Warm bread and fresh butter. There's jam on the table."

He stood and accepted the treat. His eyes caught hers, thanking her without speaking.

When she looked back a few minutes later, he was gone.

She rubbed her face at the hairline, knowing white flour would mark the gesture. Burn English hadn't changed at all.

CHAPTER ONE

The old horse lowered his head as Burn spoke to him. His fingers found the base of the ears, rubbing gently, and the stallion groaned, sighed, then nipped at Burn's arm, telling him that was enough. Burn laughed. A rare sound that sent birds flying up, and one old coyote, limping across a distant fence line, stopped and howled in answer.

"It's time, old man," Burn murmured.

The horse sighed, lower lip flapping. Burn touched the gray over the eyes, then stroked the muzzle that was almost white, where once it had been a dark brown. He slid the rope around the thick neck and fashioned a loop over the nose, in the same way he had first led the horse twenty years ago. Lamed then, a three-year-old attacked by his own sire, dying from an infected wound. Now it was age and hard use and three years of drought killing the old horse. Burn would place the shot, pull the trigger, but it was the times, the place, that confirmed the stallion's end.

Burn tugged on the rope. The stallion raised his head, looked out over the valley. They both watched the coyote slink away. The horse rubbed his head on Burn's arm and they took a step, then another, until the old horse walked with Burn, laboring over the slow rise to the hill top and the single tree waiting for them.

It took a half hour to climb the hill. Burn allowed the old horse to stop, to breathe slowly, even to nibble at the few bushes clinging in vain to the sandy soil. At the top Burn could see for miles—bright sun and clear sky, dry air. And there was nothing to ruin his view—no travelers on the roads to raise dust, no cattle being moved, no train whistling or sending its coal smoke into his world.

The stallion rubbed his head on Burn's shoulder as he loosened the nose loop. Burn let the rope slide, took it off the horse's neck, stood there silently with the animal who'd been a big part of his life for too long.

He had worried, years ago when he had first caught up the colt, that the easy temper that had allowed him to ride the youngster then would breed horses of uncertain heart. But those offspring, many of a similar quality to the bay mare, had been good using horses, quick on cattle, with plenty of endurance and easy to start, even for an old man who had broken as many bones as Burn had.

Now he laid an arm over the stallion's crest, took note of the swayed back, looked down to study the buckling knees barely able to carry the animal's expanding girth. He'd like to sit one more time on the stallion; it had been years since he had raced the horse except in his dreams. But he'd keep his promise to the end, knowing that the once sturdy body and long legs could no longer handle even his own slight weight.

Burn walked away from the hillside edge to the single tree, and, with some grumbling and complaining, the old horse followed reluctantly. When they stood in the shade, Burn went to the horse's head, brushed aside that thinning forelock, and studied the broad plane of bone with its glaring white hairs, the cavities above both eyes almost pure white, the long lashes also turned white. One finger drew a line from the base of the right ear to the top edge of the left eye; the finger's path left behind a mark of disrupted hair. He repeated the gesture from the left ear to the right eye, creating the necessary center target.

He'd buckled on a holster and belt earlier, and had been too aware of the extra, one-sided weight as he'd climbed the hill. Now he retrieved the pistol, an ancient Navy Colt that he'd earned as a kid down in Texas. He'd killed two men with it, and a panicked roan gelding. Now it would kill one more time.

The pistol was heavy. He raised it, placed it on the X made by his finger tracings, and pulled the trigger, exhaling. As the huge body fell, he shot one more time into the top of the ruined skull.

Then he turned away, went to his knees, and vomited his crude breakfast of cold coffee and stale biscuits.

The stallion's bowels had loosened. The air was foul. Burn stayed only a moment to be sure the horse was dead. Kneeling at the shattered head, he bent down, waited, held his own breath. There was nothing, no flutter of the clamped nostrils, no small puffs of dust. A trickle of blood through the clamped teeth slowed, pooling on the hard sand. No life.

He staggered down the hillside, throwing the pistol and watching it rise. It shone against the sun, then fell among the rocks and shattered, stock and metal chipping. Burn continued on, caught his boot heel, almost went down, jamming his hand into a cactus when trying to break his fall. Behind him the ravens went to work, squabbling over the excess of flesh and blood.

He was sick again when he got back to the small cabin and ended up on his knees in the paddock where the stallion had lived these past few weeks. He'd been brought in from his mares, fed extra hay. Burn had even brought home a bag of oats, but the stallion would not eat them.

Finally Burn lay on his bed, worn out, feverish, hating himself while knowing he'd done the right thing. Death was a certainty—for the stallion, and for himself.

His head jerked up and his heart began to race. He woke from the same nightmare to the sound of an approaching rider. Sitting forward, listening closely, fretful as to who would be riding up to the cabin. In his mind he could still feel the dream, but he forced himself up, went out to the porch, settled back in a chair, and watched the rider approach.

It was one of the Hildahls' kids on the bay pony, one from his old stallion crossed with a stunted mare. A good size horse and a companion for the boy; horse and rider were both from good stock, well suited to each other.

The boy's name was Henry and he came with a folded piece of paper in one hand, held out to the side as if it were on fire. Burn waited. The pony stopped at the tie rail and Henry stayed mounted, offering delivery in small movements, the paper *crackling* slightly. The bay pony cocked his head and turned one ear back but didn't shy or spook. Burn found himself smiling for the first time since his visit to Henry's mother. Here was his proof—that bay mustang sired good stock no matter what he had been bred to.

He studied Henry as if he'd never seen him before. About fifteen, tall like Davey and plain-looking, but smart, that could be seen in his eyes and his carriage. Katherine had bragged about Henry, saying he knew who he was, knew how to work hard, was good on a horse, had an instinct about where cattle hid, and, despite having grown up on a ranch, he was curious and excited about the few motorcars he'd seen. Burn guessed that when this child went from his family into the world, he'd not come back.

When Burn was the boy's age, maybe a bit older, he'd already killed two men. It made a man think how the world was changing. Burn didn't take to the new ways, not like this boy or his younger brother, Gordon. They were children of a new century, while Burn might as well be stuffed and mounted in the back room of a dusty saloon, where the doors would soon close because the patrons had gone home to their families.

Now here was Henry on that pony, holding a paper, his parents obviously asking one more thing of Burn. Good people, Katherine and Davey Hildahl, but still a demand on Burn. He leaned forward in the crude chair, put his hands on his knees, staring at the two appendages, noting the softening of the terrible scars that bound him to the Hildahls. Without their care, he would have died those years back, wrapped in the damnable barbed wire and leaking life and blood into the ground.

He could close his eyes and still see Davey's face that day. His skin pure white even though he spent most of his time under the sun, his blue eyes wet, staring at Burn who could barely feel

18

any part of himself. His own blood mingled with that of the gray horse that bled out heavily on top of him. The pain hadn't started yet, but Davey's eyes, looking down at him, had told what was coming.

Burn shook and pushed his hands between his clamped knees and the bay pony took one step back, finally unnerved. "What you want, boy?" Burn's voice cracked, a thin quiver telling of his inner wounds, but Henry wouldn't notice. He'd known Burn all his short life, Henry had. It had been Burn who had ridden for the doctor when Henry decided to be born. Katherine had come visiting to Burn's cabin, and there she'd chosen to start labor. The old man, Gayle Souter, had been visiting, too—more company than Burn had ever wanted, even though he had liked both of the folks taking up time and space in his small cabin.

Souter had birthed out his own children and Burn could ride, so there had been no discussion. The doctor was known to be at the Meiklejon house and that made Burn's ride short and sweet. He'd come back with Davey and the doctor, and had been there, walking on the porch with Davey when his wife produced their son. The hurt in Burn had grown with each gulping cry from the little one, each smile on the new papa's face, and the sweet glow from the new mother, Katherine Donald Hildahl.

He'd missed his chance, knew his loss, would

have gone right then, but he owed the newborn, owed his life to the parents, and couldn't break himself away from wanting at least to see Katherine once in a while, never for long since it grew the hurt inside, but enough to know that she was content.

He hated the Hildahls' happiness, hated the closeness between husband and wife—Burn's only real friend and the first woman, the only woman, he'd ever loved.

So he stayed for Henry, and those who had come after, even the little one who had died never having drawn a breath. He had watched Katherine's suffering, had known it wasn't for him to offer comfort, but once, in the old Meiklejon ranch house where she and Davey and their growing family lived, Katherine had put her hand on Burn's arm, had pressed down enough so he could feel each finger against the old wire scarring, and he had known what she was telling him. *We need you.* Spoken by touch, words formed but not sounded. He had nodded, keeping his own silence, and given her a brief grin, foolish on his ugly face but enough that Katherine had released him with a short laugh.

That had been ten years ago. Now it was time. He wasn't needed; he wasn't part of any life here. It had been the old horse who'd held Burn this long. He couldn't abandon the youngster deep inside the graying, tired flesh. The colt that had come to Burn when both were injured and in need.

Burn had kept his word and after that first year he never rode the colt again. The awkward youngster matured into a fine herd stallion, siring babies that looked like him and had his temperament. Burn made a good living during those years, training and selling off the four-year-olds and trading for new mares when he could.

An English-bred horse came to mean something in the southwest part of the state and even on up to Santa Fé and into Colorado where folks with too much money liked an English horse for its speed.

Now he was done. The stallion dead, his bones stripped even at this moment, coyotes howling all night as they gorged themselves, and each cry drilling Burn as his bullet had drilled through the stallion's skull. He could add that death to his legacy. His memories were filled with death, blood, gore, wounds so horrific that Burn still could not look at his own body without seeing in the rough, ridged skin across his belly and thigh what had almost killed him then, was killing him again. All those mustanging years had made him an old man at forty-five, hard-moving, slow, aching so much in the morning that getting up was a chore.

"Mister English?" Henry was being polite, asking Burn to come take the paper.

He stood finally, feeling that ancient pull across his belly from the lost battles. "Sorry, boy . . . got to thinking." He took the two steps sideways, less pain in the knees that way, and grinned to himself, probably scaring the hell out of Henry at the sight. He took the piece of paper. "Thanks, boy." Saying the boy's given name was another wound; no reason other than he was Katherine's son, born of Davey Hildahl. He wadded the paper up in his fist, knowing what it was, unable to handle the words. An invitation from the Hildahl clan to celebrate with them—a birthday, a holiday? Hell, he didn't even know what day of the week it was, never could get to a celebration on the right day. It was a standing joke that he'd shown up for Christmas a week late, one time, so they had made it a tradition to tease him as they blew whistles and brought in the New Year.

"Ain't . . . aren't you comin', Mister English? Elizabeth . . . she really wants you to be at her party . . . she's turning six this year." The child smiled and patted his bay on the shoulder. "I think she wants you to bring her a pony. I guess Mama told her about the pinto you been working with. And Elizabeth . . . she thinks it belongs to her."

Then before Burn could put the boy straight, the child kicked the bay as he reined him around, and the pony leaped into an easy lope from a spinning standstill, leaving Burn once again to regret the stallion's death.

Burn had kept a couple of the bay's sons for a while but had had offers on them too high to ignore. So he'd taken the money and put it in a bank in Socorro where it had the names of the Hildahl children on it, shared out to each as they came into the world. He hadn't told their parents yet, knowing Davey and Katherine would refuse his gift. Money wasn't much for Burn. He could always ride a horse and get a meal, a barn for the night. $5,000 was more than he could understand.

But a child, or three, four maybe, they could use that to go to college back East where all education was fancy and important, or, now, maybe to the coast of California where cities were growing back after that awful earthquake, and all kinds of knowledge could be learned. It would have to be paid for, and Burn knew the earnings of a ranch foreman didn't allow for the proper education of four children.

The dust of the bay pony's departure settled. Burn eased back into the chair, rested those outsize and wounded hands on his knees, and worked at thinking, seeing ahead of him a new road promised across his land, poles and wires going up so folks could talk to each other without going outside the door, saddling or harnessing a horse, and making an effort to visit.

Burn didn't want talking most of the time. Once

in a while he'd spoken of his feelings with Davey, after that terrible wire accident, and then the facedown with an outlaw gone bad, but, since then, well, Davey'd married Katherine and there was no time for easy talk between friends.

He stood up, tired of thinking back, needing to do what had been tormenting him for months. The stallion's destruction finally would get him moving.

In the corral he had a draft team, steady monsters that could pull anything a man wanted moved. He'd used their mama and a sorrel gelding, borrowed from Meiklejon, to pull the cabin from its old spot to where it was now so that he could look out and see the valley and nothing else. That team was long gone to bone and dust, and the valley was crowded so that a man saw houses and wagons and once in a while one of those motorcars, honking and belching and scaring the chickens.

But he still had his draft team and he'd use them one more time. Burn was slow and deliberate hitching them—Bill on the left, Jake always on the right. They worked better that way. Matched sorrels they were—their sire a big old boy from up in Albuquerque that the owner said was a Belgian. Fancy papers or home-grown, Burn didn't care. The two geldings did their work and more, and occasionally Burn and the team hired out to work for other folks, doing their clearing, plowing, or skidding rafter logs from a distant stand of straight pine.

The first pull on the corral gatepost sent the sorrel geldings to their knees. The damned thing was in deep, but it still was only wood, and the team leaned their considerable weight and stubborn tempers into the task. With a low sigh the gatepost twitched, shivered, and then split apart, tumbling the attached rails that brought down more posts and then railings until the whole prison rolled violently apart like broken tree limbs. Burn laughed as he slapped the team into a brisk trot to get them out of any possible danger.

This time when he reined them around and asked them to back up, it was to the pitch of the cabin. With the chain hooked inside the front door, the team barely had to jerk forward to bring down the loosened boards, old and dried out. The roof quickly collapsed, dust rolling over Burn and Bill and Jake. The house was gone, old history buried. That done, he unhitched the team, letting the harness lay where it fell once stripped from the sweaty bodies as if the animals wearing that leather and metal had disappeared, leaving behind only the outline of their working lives.

He had his shoeing tools away from the barn, nested with his saddle, bridle, saddle blanket, and all the gear he would need. He had put them there this morning, after feeding the three remaining horses. The others had been turned out last night.

Now there was only the dark bay mare that looked a lot like her daddy. He'd deliberated about keeping the mule for packing, but he'd changed his mind this morning, so he'd already turned the mule loose. Left the mare alone, set her up for being fretful.

It took him just moments to pull the team's shoes that were shod only on the front hoofs to prevent against bruising from stones in their work. He rasped the hoofs even, set each one down—a job well done, and for the last time. He pulled off the bridles, those damned blinkers stirring up dust where he dropped them. The team stood quietly, close to each other, waiting to be told what to do. It took Burn slapping Bill on the hindquarters to get the big son moving, with Jake trailing along a half stride from his teammate.

He watched the simple thought process go through the team's mind. Nothing held them, nothing on their head, no fence around them, nothing to stop them. Finally Bill lumbered into his heavy trot and Jake followed. Bill reached over and nipped at his buddy. Jake squealed and half bucked, and then the two horses broke into a gallop that shook the ground.

Burn was still laughing as the air slowly settled. In the distance was a long trail of high dust, one sharp whinny, and then the team was gone. Burn turned his attention to the rest of the plan.

The older brood mares, he'd let them go with

their foals. They'd either drift into the wild life or be caught, branded with another rancher's mark. He had no geldings—all sold and gone, the money in that bank account, a few dollars in his back pocket. No stud colts, none of them could replace their sire.

Word would get out quickly, hurried along by Henry's visit and the rejected invitation, and the appearance of the well-known English brand on hides throughout Datil and Red Hill and over to the plains of San Agustin. The wandering horses would come up against barbed wire and know to follow the fence line instead of fighting it.

It was more than Burn had known—that damned wire had nearly killed him.

CHAPTER TWO

Alone, the bay mare was nervous in the small, side pen—head up, eyes too white, sweating along her neck and at her loins. She paced the fence, muzzle skimming the top rail. She stopped several times to whinny for Bill . . . Jake.

Burn went in the pen and the mare ran from him, head still high, eyes still showing too much white. He decided that maybe he'd kept the wrong horse, or that he should have thought to hold Bill and Jake until the mare was saddled and ready. When he finally caught her, using soft words and a light rope laid over her neck, he spent a few moments soothing her—a soft brush, his hands on her hide—gently rubbing her muzzle until the tight hold of her lips softened and she finally yawned, dropped her head, and rubbed against him.

He called her Beauty despite an old reluctance to name his horses. Her sire had been nameless except in the beginning, when Burn had called him Jester because he was sure the colt was always playing tricks on him. That name had slipped away as he rode the dark bay hard the long summer of being chased, herding a few mares, ducking the law and angry ranchers. The colt had saved his life over and over, so the name was buried, given away to the wind, and the stallion had nothing to bind him to human need or Nature except to reproduce himself as often as possible.

As Burn slipped the simple jointed bit into the mare's mouth, he braided a long strand of black hair across the brow band carefully as the mare tossed her head before quieting. It was all that remained of her father's physical presence. Too sentimental, too foolish for Burn, but he had taken the strand while the stallion was alive, receiving a peculiar look from the dark bay as he had lifted the black tail and used his knife to cut out the shank of hair. He had needed something more than the legacy of the bay's offspring.

He had everything ready—saddlebags and a bedroll, a good sheepskin coat, a thick black hat and gloves, even a scarf. He was riding north this time, out of the New Mexico Territory. It was going to be a state soon if the politicos up in Santa Fé had their way—a state defined with roads and poles and electricity—and Burn was going north to where maybe he could find a place no one else wanted to be.

He guided the mare through a series of small cañons and valleys, places he knew were free of wire. In the saddlebags were wire cutters and short pieces of wire, and to carry them was illegal, but he didn't care. If he came up against the damned wire—and he would—a quick cut, a wrap he'd done many times, and he'd go through on to the next wire fence that needed cutting. He would make the repairs tight, not wanting to stir up trouble because of his passing.

Word would travel quickly that his place was gone, corral and house destroyed, and eventually the bank in Socorro would let Davey know about the college money and that he now owned the rough 4,000 acres Burn had earned through the horses. An easy transfer, with the banker sworn to remain silent, but Burn had faith in the man's soft conscience, and, when enough time had passed, when word got spread around down into Gutierrezville and Alma and even down the Río

Grande Valley to Hot Springs and up to Belen—all in the territory of New Mexico—the banker would be glad to talk, to tell the few curious folks what he'd known all along, and here was what he knew.

Katherine might take a moment to think of him, maybe even to cry, and then Davey would hold her and they'd be with each other again without Burn to watch and be hurt over their constant affection. He valued their place in his life, but being near them kept him wounded and it was a damned fool thing for an old *mesteñero* to accept as his only life.

He hoped most of the horses, even the sorrel team of Bill and Jake, would escape capture, would travel as they chose and eat the sweet grasses, stand in the deep shade, head to tail, to swish away pestering flies, trusting each other for comfort and safety.

He let the mare shift into her easy lope. She came up light in the bridle, used her hindquarters, and it felt more natural to him than sitting on the porch in that damned rocker that the fat old man from his past had left him. The old man had died under the name of Eager Briggs, but Burn had remembered his real name. Riding a good horse was better than any soft-padded chair or thick mattress. It was a lope carrying him out of a life he had never wanted, except for that one woman.

• • •

Burn judged the line he chose as straight north, always staying west of the Río Grande Valley. There were times when he and Beauty topped a rise and he could follow the river's dry course by the richness of the yellowed cottonwood leaves. First thing a man learns in dry country—to judge water by the luxury of the trees.

He stayed close to the old fence line Meiklejon had put up, the first fence in the area, eighteen years ago. He still hadn't run into much of the wire yet, except for the railroad tracks coming from Socorro into Magdalena. He'd keep west of there, to avoid getting tangled in the right of way and all that damned wire. Four miles, straight north, to his first fence. Once there, he climbed down, dropped the reins. The mare insisted on rubbing her face on his back while he snipped the five strands of wire. This time it was easy. A lazy ranch hand had left coiled wire nearby, so Burn didn't need to use any of the strands he had brought along. He'd counted on this sloppy habit to make repairs.

He led the mare through the opening, the cut wire carefully dragged to one side. But when a strand rattled, the mare cocked her head and turned skittish, and only then did he remember that she and her mama'd been caught in wire once. Beauty had been maybe two months old, so the scar had slowly disappeared, but not the fear.

He rubbed between her eyes, laid an arm over her neck, and she walked past the wire, trembling but without further trouble.

It took him a good half hour to rewire, and he knew why. He felt the mare's fear in his own wrist and fingers, deep in his gut, and he almost was sick from the chore. Damned fools, both of them, him and the mare. As he mounted and Beauty tried to bolt, Burn figured he'd chosen the right horse for his leaving. She had his fears and for the same reasons.

Beneath him, under hide and behind bone and ligament, a heart beat too fast, mimicking his own reaction, so Burn let the mare pick her pace. This time it was a run, hard on Burn, so he stood in the stirrups, held to the saddle swell, and let her go. As she slowed, Burn rode down into the saddle seat and felt the years poke and prod him. Pain was a familiar constant. This time, though, heading out to whatever would become his end, he found agony rode inside him, more intense than the simple morning pain he usually felt.

Finally he had to stop the mare and climb down and lean over. He coughed up blood, thin mucus, some liquid. Mostly blood. He'd felt it more than six months ago when he rode his last bronco, a deep palomino stallion left too long unbroken. It had been a hard ride. He'd come off twice, and each time the owner and his men had laughed as if the bucking son-of-a-bitch was a toy any child could handle. He had reminded them later, when the stallion was walking and trotting on command, coming to a good stop, even backing a step or two, that they'd brought the horse to him because they couldn't do their own dirty work at home.

The rancher had nodded thoughtfully and offered Burn an extra $10. He'd refused, taking the $20 they'd bargained on, saying it was enough.

He'd known the truth then, and nothing had healed since, nothing had gotten better, and he had had to shoot an old horse, and now he couldn't let a smooth-gaited mare have a run without cutting himself more inside. He was tired of the whole mess, including the mess he'd made of his life. God damn.

He let the mare drift while keeping the valley to his right, not a line but a boundary he would not cross. The shadows drew away from the mare's hoofs, leaving spindly marks and exaggerated strides. He laughed. The mare cranked one ear back and Burn lightly touched her neck. Colors startled him as he passed one of the looming hills—a vivid red sky, a richer color than what he'd seen on an apple or the sweaters Katherine had knitted for her blonde daughters. Finally the colors faded to the softness of Katherine's skin when she blushed, or stood near her husband. Then the blue came, starting out thin under the clouds, changing, then thickening to a dark layer that was black. Burn slapped his thigh and knew the feel of his hand on cured hide. He wore his old mustanger chaps, the second pair he'd made and worn through in that year of chasing down the wild herd that had become the foundation for his time as a breeder of horses.

He counted them, totaled up the years. Seventeen it had taken him to leave since their wedding ceremony where he'd stood up next to Davey and made a jackass of himself, blushing and stammering. He'd never been in any one place in his life that long; now he was a man with no skills, no money, and nothing holding him down.

There was a soothing rhythm to constant movement, a release from responsibility, owing no one and free to ride on. It came back to him— the day not that long ago when he had left Katherine for the last time, carrying a slice of her fresh bread mounded with butter and jam, made from berries the children had picked high up in the mountains. He'd almost forgotten, with all the civilizing forces around him—children and a home—the horses that depended on him.

Now he understood that Katherine had made the right choice. He'd have been no companion for such a woman. The knowing had freed him and he had put together his plan. Now he was gone.

When he realized the sky was dark gray and no

more shadows slipped under the mare's tracks, it registered that he needed to make camp. The careful habits came back easily—strip and hobble the mare, feed her a handful of oats from the saddlebags, tie his gear up into a stunted juniper, and camp close to it so no critter would come around, hunting salt. A dry camp tonight. He'd share water from the canteen with the mare, knowing tomorrow there would be a spring or stream. He'd been headed in the right direction, but hadn't paid much attention to how far out he still was.

Hunger got taken care of by a fry pan of beans, thirst went before an airtight of peaches, the juice sticking to his fingers as he knived through the tin top, a skill he'd once possessed, now lost but coming back, as he let his fingers feel the raw edge, knowing how to use the blade. The juice was perfect and he licked the inside of the airtight, careful not to cut his tongue. He could easily eat another one of these treats, but food would become a problem quick enough and Burn knew he didn't have the edge left to go for days on water and biscuits and a cold camp. Soft now, a long time living with human comforts—an outhouse and water pump, a wood stove, a mattress set over a rope-strung frame. Comforts he couldn't bring with him, didn't want any more.

He knew he was lying to himself. He wanted those and more, but she had never come to him,

35

never left her husband and family, only smiled at him and sent over peach preserves or a salted ham and invited him for the holidays he had forgotten.

Sad affair for him. No choice now but to ride out and find something, almost anything, to keep himself alive, or ride on into the distance where life and death merged. He didn't much care. It wasn't a wish or a hope, but simply the reality that came smacking him on the nose with that birthday invitation and a child wanting a paint pony that wasn't ever going to do for her. He couldn't have looked into that pretty face, so much like her ma's, and told the child no. Never.

He had run from a six-year-old and a growing hatred of the life he had come to accept, and the ache put in his gut from the last bucking horse he'd rode, and years filled with too many of them, with all the bucking horses. He was torn apart, both in his belly and his heart, and it had been time to get free of those wounds.

He was headed north, by God, and he needed sleep. Even the bay mare was dozing maybe ten feet away, head down, tail barely moving, eyes half closed. She'd keep watch. Burn could sleep now, knowing he was safe.

The ground was hard, the sky too bright. He rolled over and a rock dug into his hip. He groaned, and the mare whinnied at him, which made him laugh. At least something was funny.

He'd kept his old rifle cleaned and oiled. Now

he lay on the ground, counting the coyote howls and thinking about struggling to get up and maybe firing into the empty night, scaring the sons-of-bitches who would ruin his first free sleep. They kept howling, but finally he went to sleep flat on his back, half out of the bedroll, boots near his head, the rifle just out of reach.

He could tell by the stars. How much they'd moved. Something had awoken him. He grabbed for the weapon, sat up, and spooked the mare that was standing over him. It was more, though, not her presence, but an extra sound. A growl, a metal *rattle*. He scrambled upright, and, bent over with the rifle, he headed toward the sound.

He found a varmint with its head in the airtight. Peaches, just the scent of them, would do that to a varmint, and a starving man, too. Burn managed to straighten up, and, even while he was laughing, he caught the long tail—a raccoon—which was reasonable, and he held onto the tail while trying to pull the can loose. The raccoon wasn't too pleased with getting his butt kicked while he couldn't see. Burn was of the opinion that if the varmint would hold still for only a moment, he could get that damned can off, and they could part in a friendly manner.

But it wasn't going to happen, so Burn stepped on the raccoon's neck just behind the ears pinned inside the can and that stopped the thrashing somewhat but not the squalling echo from inside the can. Then the damned varmint pissed on one of Burn's bare feet, spread wide to balance as he pulled and yanked and swore. Exactly what he'd feared, of course, happened. The raccoon's head slid free and Burn fell backward, foot covered in raccoon piss, and the varmint sat up, paws waving, that black-masked face grinning in the clear early morning sky, and Burn got a good scolding for his wayward treatment of a poor animal just trying to keep on living.

Burn stood up and the raccoon sauntered away, ringed tail trailing behind him, leaving Burn with a stink and a belly aching with laughter.

After he'd rubbed sand on his foot to rid himself of the raccoon smell, he crawled into his blankets. The hobbled mare was some distance from him and she kept watching his struggle to slide in, rest the rifle nearby, draw the blankets to his chin. The night air was chilly. Then Burn was asleep.

The mare snorted and squealed as something kicked Burn in the side. He rolled away, tangled for a moment in his blanket, then, scrambling free, grabbed the rifle and came up rifle in hand, hammer cocked. No point in waiting. Whatever had kicked him needed to know he was ready.

"What the hell you doing in our pasture?" The voice was huge, but Burn didn't look up at it.

There were other shapes drifting between him and the mare, and, when she kicked one of them and it cursed, Burn grinned.

"Sleeping, you damned fool! Can't you tell when a man's sleeping?" A different voice, and coming from the same direction.

Burn got his bearings, kept the hammer back, the rifle pointed to the ground. He was surprised they'd given him the chance. It was his warning to the bastards, and the circle of men seemed to read what he was telling them. He could feel his gut turn, tasting bitter blood, and he was getting mad enough to shoot any one of these rannies who tried moving toward him.

They seemed to know that, also. It was in their eyes. Hell, Burn thought, he wasn't far enough from his old grounds that these boys didn't know his reputation. One of the old ones, the fool *mesteñero* folks talked about.

He could see clearly now. His eyes focused on one or two of the intruders—the big one who stood back, and the smaller, younger son-of-a-bitch who had to have been the kicker. It showed in his face, that eagerness to stir trouble.

Burn circled the rifle barrel until it was aimed at the boy's middle—the easiest shot guaranteed to bring a man down. The boy knew that, and so did the men standing nearby. Slowly, hands held wide, they drifted so it was only the boy facing Burn and his rifle. The weapon might be old and out of date, not fancy or engraved, but in Burn's hands, shaky maybe with anger and fear, its threatening message was clear.

The rifle was heavy in Burn's hand. He hadn't fired a shot in years except for killing the stallion. There was *that* leftover taste in him, of powder and death that he hadn't outrun yet. This kid, kicking him for no damned good reason, made him downright ornery.

The big man spoke and the boy eased back.

The rifle was getting heavier, but Burn wasn't ready to lower it, to give the boy any peace of mind.

"Name's Warren Hardesty, Mister English. We surely didn't know it was you. . . . Thought you'd head south this time a year."

Burn wanted to wipe his sweating face but the kid had a mean eye.

"We've been having troubles on this land," Hardesty explained. "Some folks down by the river . . . well, they think this is their private hunting preserve. Ray here, he's been taking care of chasing them off the land. He gets a mite pushy at times, but we sure as hell didn't mean to interrupt your sleep. Just didn't know who you were."

Something caught Burn's eye and he began to laugh. "You boys're riding my stock. All o' you."

"Yes, sir, Mister English. And the boss wants to

know what we'll do now you seem bent on leaving."

Burn was just curious enough to ask: "Who's your boss?"

"Ron Platten of the Cross B."

Burn nodded. Platten had bought a lot of his best horses over the years. Burn said: "Tell him Frank Wainright, over to Springerville, has a son of the old stallion. He's been coming up with some nice colts."

Even with all the friendly talk, Burn kept the old rifle pointed at the boy's gut.

Finally the big man, Hardesty, asked for a truce. Burn agreed, but only if the kid stepped back to hold the horses and stayed in Burn's line of sight. He wanted to keep an eye on him but didn't want him part of any more talk.

The boy moved back with Hardesty's thick forearm helping him along. "You say Frank's got some of your bloodstock?" Hardesty said, trying to keep Burn's attention. When Burn nodded, Hardesty asked: "You have any say in the mares?"

That was a surprising question. Most ranchers figured it was all from the stallion.

"Yeah," Burn answered. "I sent along a few I thought he could use. We talked a bit. I told him my thinking on the type of mare needed. Guess he's got a good strain going." It was more than Burn usually said to a stranger, but it was about

41

horses, his horses, his only legacy. He turned his back to Hardesty, speaking quickly as he went to the bay mare who was trying to hop away. "You all said what you needed to say. Got me up too god-damn' early, and now my horse's trying to leave without me. Gentlemen, that's enough."

Polite for him, but too wordy. He walked away, rifle still in his hand. At one point he raised the rifle over his head as a reminder. Mutterings behind him, a sharp word, a saddle *jingle,* horses farting, and then it was quiet and he had his hands on the mare, who sighed and rubbed her head on his shoulder. Burn had to take her mane and just above her nostrils and lead her forcibly back to the camp. Then he bridled the mare, loosened her hobbles, watered her from his punched hat, and tied her to the juniper.

The riders were gone except for their dust and a few piles of fresh manure, boot prints, and a present in his blankets—balls of wet manure kicked there. The boy's parting shot.

He wished he had had the *cojones* to pull the trigger, fire at their retreating backs, but he couldn't afford wasting a bullet.

CHAPTER THREE

Burn was three hours in the saddle and it was getting hot out on the flatlands. Dusty, empty, no fences, no nothing until he saw that lick of yellow flame that told him the trees he'd seen yesterday were showing off their water. He and the mare were dry, so he didn't have to lay the rein lightly on her neck, just simply look at the distant trees. Four of them he counted, a good sign, and the mare lit into that easy lope headed straight to the spot Burn was thinking about.

It had been more than twenty-four hours with only one canteen between them. Burn slid off the mare as she slowed to a hard stop and let himself fall into the water, burying his head, blowing water from his mouth, then rolling over and resting his head in the water, looking up at the close sky, listening to the mare snorting and blowing and doing her own wallowing. He spat out one last dribble of water, then rolled himself up and squatted. He washed his hands, ducked his head under again, laughing as he swallowed and coughed and swallowed again. Then he remembered last night and shucked off his right boot, pulled the sock free, ducked his foot in the water, using sand to scrub the flesh. There was no more stink now, nothing but the memory of that miserable raccoon and his opinion of Burn's efforts at rescue.

The bay mare lifted her head and whinnied. Burn scrambled to his feet, hobbling on his naked foot as he reached for the rifle stuck in its scabbard. One hand touching the grip, he settled, listened, heard what the mare already had sensed. More horses. Hell, a man couldn't ride even a half day without meeting up with the whole damned territory.

Burn let go of the rifle butt, loosened the rope from the other side of the horn, and started swinging it lightly. The mare winced, ducked her head, but kept her ears pricked while Burn watched in the direction from where the sound came.

It was nothing more than a band of horses coming up quickly. The singing rope had slowed them considerably, but one dark colt came on ahead.

Burn threw out the rope, intending to miss, but, instead of bolting, the colt struck out at it. Burn laughed as he read the brand. He remembered this one, bold and aggressive with the bad eye of his mama. He'd not wanted to breed the mare, or keep her, but Davey had asked, as a favor, and Burn had given in reluctantly. Then he had tried to get Davey to geld the colt, but Davey had sold it as a weanling, telling the buyer to geld him.

The man hadn't yet, most likely wouldn't, and he'd be getting fractious offspring and blaming Burn for not having told the truth. A man didn't want to see that eye and that lean gut. Not meant for a stallion, and he wouldn't hardly be worth the cost of a worn-out livery bronco.

This colt had his mama's fire. She had been an old mare Davey had bought out of pity. This was her last colt, and he was a hell raiser. Temperament ran in families, just as athletic ability and even spookiness. He'd known when he sold the colt, it had been a bad bargain.

It was obvious what was pushing the young stallion. He arched his neck and whickered low, prancing now, his flaccid organ swinging, but his intent clear. Burn was being challenged by the colt for rights to Beauty.

Burn laughed, coiled in the rope, and threw it, hitting the colt's nose and stopping the charge. He quickly coiled the rope again and slapped it against his chaps, yelling. The horses scattered in a slow trot, taking the colt reluctantly with them.

Then Burn was ready to sit down and pull on the damp sock and the boot, once it was shaken free of dust and pebbles. His foot didn't feel like some animal's main dumping ground any more. He actually laughed as he checked the mare's *cincha* and mounted up, easing the mare into her smooth walk, heading north.

He rode a week or more, skirting around any of the larger towns like Albuquerque, barely seeing the smoke from the village of Santa Fé. He managed a high trail alongside the Río Grande but had to cross over when the gorge narrowed and the land got serious. He'd taken a silent oath on the remains of the cabin that he would ride the west side of the river only, but he'd never been this far north and the river water got narrow and rough. In several places the mare balked, being more level-headed than Burn, so he turned her back around and followed a simple path that took him to a wide place in the river where the tracks told him it was safe to cross.

That was a long day. Burn ate a lot of humble pie. The mare proved smarter than her rider, and he found admitting to that flaw a sour experience. What he did realize after that long week was a lessening of the blood he was spitting up. So he guessed that leaving home at his age had been the right thing for his health.

Along the river he stopped at small villages, where he became a cause for excitement. The crowds unnerved Burn, but the mare seemed to delight in the small hands patting her and offering delights such as crystal sugar and sometimes fresh grass pulled from a farmer's pasture. A hot meal, pasture for the mare, a nest in the barn were offered and accepted. He couldn't figure out what these folks got out of their generosity; he had no talents or skills, or money, to share with them.

Mostly the village men seemed to tend sheep or grow a few crops. The women worked the homes. The children ran and played. It was a good life, simple and clean and enticing to a lonesome man with no place to go. But then he would encounter one of those motorcars, sputtering through the narrowed roads, scraping at the walls in places where fences grew close to the track, where neighbors spoke to each other over the adobe walls, and there wasn't room for the width and stink of a motorcar. But still they came, their drivers delighting in honking and scattering everything around them.

With each kindness provided him, Burn knew well enough to say his thank you. After all these years his mama's voice still came to him, clearly directing his manners. It would be said first to the woman of the house who had kindly fed him, then to the husband whose generosity had kept him safe through the night. Finally a touch to the heads of the younger children, a nod to the older boys, barely a glance at the older girls, and he was gone, to be met at the next village with the same kindnesses.

He guessed he was an outdated oddity, a *gringo* on horseback, looking scruffy and old, riding a fine young mare that the men in these villages talked about as if she were magic. He knew her perfection—the glossy mane and tail, the smallest of white on her face between her nostrils, an anklet of white around both her hind coronet bands. Her steps were strong and even. She rarely stumbled through the worst of rock-strewn areas or fallen trees, and the small woods animals, the prairie creatures did not upset her with their quick intrusions. It was only right that the men in these villages appreciated her worth. It made a man feel proud to ride such a fine animal, even if she was a mare.

On several occasions he saw motorcars out in the open. He'd seen them on the road across his land a number of times, and he'd run into one in Socorro that scared the young buckskin he was riding. The bronco had had a pitching fit. Burn had managed to stay aboard, but once again had a feeling deep in his belly that he couldn't take this any more.

He was running from the picture he had seen in his nightmares of doing an old man's work, struggling just to survive. It wasn't for him, that decline of strength, skill, even the ability to see being marred by a film across old eyes. He'd ridden at death too often to let it slowly creep into his belly and spread outward.

Along the river above Santa Fé, he was letting the mare graze as she walked. He wrapped one leg around the saddle horn and was half sleeping, feeling the warmth along the back of his neck, hearing the river's flow. Enjoying the day. Suddenly the mare lurched to a stop. Burn quickly went for the rifle as he stuck his boot back in the off stirrup. Then he heard it, a growling, joined by other threatening sounds, and a high voice, cries, then more growling. He drove the mare toward the sound, jamming his hat down, loosening the rifle to be ready.

It was two children—small boys—circled by a pack of dogs. Yellow and red dogs, tails shivering, growling, creeping closer to the children. The bigger boy threw a stone and hit one of the dogs. It howled and whined as the others drew near it, then all began stalking the children again.

Burn slid off the mare as one of the boys cried to him: "Help us! They will not go away!" Then, just as Burn saw the blood: "One bit my sister . . . she's bleeding."

Burn barely needed to aim the rifle before he shot, lifting the rifle just high enough to hit ribs, spines. The curs howled, snapping at their wounds. One went down and lay still. The others ran as Burn kept firing. Then the children screamed and he felt a tear at his left arm. He looked sideways to find one of the dogs biting down on bone, holding fast, and growling. He used his right arm to slam the rifle butt against the cur's jaw—hard enough that he heard bone break as the animal fell off, struggling to run away. Burn aimed the rifle and fired. The animal dropped, its hind legs frozen. Then it laid its head down in the sand and coughed once before dying.

The children ran toward him. Burn knelt, catching them as they hit his chest. He held them, feeling their thin bodies. Then he pushed them back, turned to the girl—it was a girl, no doubt—whose face was bleeding below the eye. Her wails hurt him. He touched her face and the cries increased.

The boy spoke then, defending his sister. "You will take us home. Mama will take care of her." The boy was a man then, only a child of eight or nine, but a man taking care of his sister. Until he, too, began to cry again, pleading: "Take us home!"

There was a shirt in Burn's saddlebags and he gave it to the little girl, wadding it in her hand and suggesting she hold it to her face. She did not look at Burn, but stared at her brother until he nodded and told her to do what the strange man said.

He lifted them onto the mare's back, both of them fitting into the saddle seat, and instructed the boy to hold his sister with one hand and the saddle horn with the other.

The boy was insulted. "I have my own pony and I can ride alone."

Burn tried a grin. "I know, but your sister needs help staying in that saddle. It's bigger'n she is."

The boy seemed to understand the good sense and immediately grabbed onto his sister.

The mare walked very carefully, and the little girl's cries slowed, then stopped. Burn looked up to study the children's faces. They were Anglo, with blond hair and blue eyes, unusual in this part of New Mexico.

The boy needed no prodding, giving Beauty directions, right and left, until they entered the yard of a small ranch, more of a farm. There were crops near the edge of a ditch and a few cattle and one mule grazing in the high grass.

A woman ran from the house, calling out a man's name—"Ed! Ed!"—and then crying for her children. Her voice was shrill yet it brought some life into the girl, who dropped the soaked cloth and held out her arms to her mama. The woman shoved her way past Burn and grabbed the child down from the saddle, holding her close until she realized the wound was bleeding again. Her face was vivid as she glared at Burn. "What did you do to my child?"

Burn had no answer. Mouth open, he tried to get out a few words, but the woman went on about her precious daughter until the boy tugged on her arm and said: "It was Ulrich's dogs, Mama. The she-dog and her puppies . . . only they grew up and they hurt Missy and wanted to eat me. This man . . . he shot them, and now Ulrich's going to kill us."

The woman grunted a few words and dragged her children into the house.

Burn waited with the mare.

Several minutes passed, and then the woman stuck her head outside again. "You, mister, get in here. My husband's coming up from the field."

Burn slowly wrapped the mare's reins around a tie rail at the front of the yard. He spent a moment touching the mare's neck, loosening her *cincha*, not wanting to be in the house until the husband had made it up from the fields.

Only when he knocked at the door and was told to enter did he begin to feel the effect of the dog bite. His arm throbbed and he could feel blood dripping onto his pants, off the ends of his fingers. His hand was numb, but the bite hurt like hell. He banged up against a wall, cursing.

The husband arrived at that moment, speaking out harshly. "We do not talk so in this house. You will not curse in front of our children!" When his wife explained the situation, he said: "We have you to thank for our children not being further mangled. We are in your debt, sir."

It was a peculiar family, Burn decided. There he stood bleeding onto their carefully swept wood floor and he was getting lectured on his speech. He was his own man, and he figured he could say what he wanted. Then he saw the big eyes of the girl child, the one he'd first thought was a boy. Her hair was cut short, and she was dressed in britches and a loose shirt, but her face was female all right, pouting mouth and tears filling the huge blue eyes. She was held by her mother, while the bite was washed, a cloth now pressed against the wound so that it would begin to clot.

Burn figured he should keep his mouth shut for the time being. The little girl was brave, and he'd better be able to do the same. He turned toward the father, Ed. The man was tall, heavy through the chest and shoulder. His head butted forward as if looking for a fight. Burn sighed. He'd stepped into a place he didn't want to be. But then he couldn't have left the children to that pack of dogs.

"Your son said the dogs belonged to a man name of Ulrich," Burn said. "He gonna give you trouble? I can go tell him I done the shooting . . . but those dogs. . . ."

Ed raised a large hand. "We will not speak of the transgressions of Mister Ulrich. He has harmed our family. I will take Providence's urging and deal with the matter with my own hand." Ed held himself steady, hardly blinking.

The man was a believer, a Bible-spouter, and Burn's general reaction to such men was to turn around and run like hell. He almost stated these sentiments out loud, except he glanced at the child's eyes, which stared at him as if expecting retribution. Instead, he smiled at the child, half raised his arm. The little girl began wailing even though her mama was holding her.

It took a moment but the words she cried out became clear to Burn.

"He's bleeding like me. Mama help him!" The child struggled in her mother's arms, determined to be put down. Her movements reopened her wound and a thin trickle of blood ran down her face, mixing with her tears, and creating a pale pink streak down the front of her shirt.

Then shyly she went to Burn, holding out one hand to touch his wounded arm. He knelt, letting her small fingers stroke the bloody sleeve. Then there was a feather touch, a bare grazing of open skin. He winced. He couldn't stop his body from reacting, and the little girl withdrew her touch.

"Sir, I will bathe that wound," said the woman. "I might have to take a few stitches, for the dog appears to have opened quite a gap in the muscle." She hesitated, and her husband took over the conversation.

"When my wife has seen to your injuries, I expect you will wish to ride on. We have little enough, but we will provide you with victuals for your journey, and perhaps a handful of grain for that mare you ride. It is the best we can do."

Somehow in all the speechifying Burn perceived an echo of dislike, almost anger that he had appeared to rescue their children. He was obviously not of the quality of folk they preferred to have enter through their door.

Burn grinned, figuring it was the one silent

gesture that would irritate the sour husband and father. It wasn't easy for Burn—being rough on a man protecting his own, but the fancy manner, kind of like Gordon Meiklejon at his worst, rubbed wrong against Burn. He opened his mouth, but then shut it, only nodding to the man.

The wife directed him to sit down in a hard-slatted chair near the table. She picked up the pan and poured out the water used for her daughter and splashed in fresh hot water, asking the boy to gather up new cloths. Then she proceeded to tear the sleeve off Burn's shirt before he could protest, and began the painful course of cleaning the wound, pouring on more hot water until the wound pulsed and Burn would have preferred to lie down.

The faces of the two children gave him strength, and, when he smiled at the little girl, she giggled and put two fingers into her mouth. The cut beneath her eye glistened with white skin, a few droplets of blood.

The woman spoke directly into Burn's ear, as if hiding the words from her husband, who tended to the fire in the cook stove. "I would give you whiskey for this, but Edvard does not allow spirits in the house, not even for medicinal purposes."

They were a pair, he thought, as she stitched through his flesh, wincing herself with each pull of the needle as if she could take away the pain. They wanted purity and perfection as they worked the land. Taking pleasure in the marriage bed would be a sin for them, he decided, and found himself feeling sorry for the woman, remembering Katherine's delighted smile whenever Davey came close.

The arm ached and pinched, but Burn held himself tightly, refusing to give in to the pain. The woman quickly wrapped a long white cloth around the wound, and he was able, by lifting his arm, to see the neatly tucked end.

"There, mister. . . ." It showed in her face— dismay and fear. It was her husband's shadow over her, his bulk seeming to push her down. The big voice rumbled from his chest, and Burn had to fight another grin, knowing it would make it harder on the woman after he left.

"You never told us your name." Almost an accusation, as if Burn were the trouble here, not a distant neighbor and a pack of unruly dogs.

He managed to stand, despite feeling light-headed. "My name is Burn English, but I don't know your name, mister. Or the names of your children . . . and wife." That seemed to confuse the man, for he stammered his answer.

"My name is Edvard Robey. This is my wife Ardith, and our children are Edvard and Henrietta." He hesitated. "We call her Missy."

Ardith had known only Edvard, had been bound to him when she was fifteen by her parents. Their family farm in Illinois could not carry the seven daughters and four sons born to them, so the daughters were given to any man showing an interest. Ardith had been scared of Edvard, until they finally came together in their marriage bed, where she found him to be fearful and shy. Having grown up on the farm with brothers and animals had helped her guide her husband through a natural process, which had produced five children. The three oldest were married and gone; the younger two had come when Ardith was turning into an old woman of forty, and they were her delight even as they exhausted her. But for the rare occasion, Edvard had since fore-sworn the marriage bed and turned to his Bible, his nightly readings often ending in a sermon delivered to Ardith as they lay side-by-side in bed.

Now he stood towering over the compact man who had delivered their children safely home. Edvard's face showed his inward battle between the rage always within easy reach of his tongue and fists, and the Christian sense of duty to a stranger. It was a swift battle, Ardith already knowing Edvard's response. The husband set out his hand, shook Burn's, which was almost the size of Edvard's fist, and then slammed out the back door to go to the barn to continue the never ending chore of cleaning out manure that vexed him even as it gave a outlet for his excessive energy and strength.

Words of thanks were never uttered. Tonight, Ardith knew, would be a monument to her husband's torment. He would take her, after much prayer and sermonizing, and she would find delight in the roughness of his skin, the closeness of his flesh. He may have given away his right to their union, but she had not made that promise. It took the internal rage of such happenings as the wound to Henrietta's face to force Edvard into a need great enough that he would foreswear his oath and use his wife as their God intended.

Burn had no idea why the woman smiled as her husband bolted from their home. The handshake had been a quick contest—one Burn had not lost or won. He was betting the man had run because Burn had not been the weaker of the two. It made a man that size plumb ornery to be stood up to by a runt like Burn. He'd known that reaction most of his life. At first it had led to fights, but now he was able to laugh at anyone thinking he would be the weaker. Some folks sure were set on their judgments; this big man had a case of hate and Burn was ready to be gone.

Ardith's smile dimmed as she busied herself with picking up foodstuffs and shoving them into a burlap sack. Burn made no attempt to stop her, especially when she put a whole loaf of bread into a second sack. He could taste it, with fresh butter and jam, and it was the memory of the last time he had seen Katherine and not what this woman was doing that flooded over him, and for now he'd accept that fantasy.

"Here." Ardith handed him two bags, a good size load for a woman of her age and tiredness.

"Thank you, ma'am . . . Miz Robey. Ma'am, you got a shirt some smaller than what your husband might wear . . . an old one, or something needs patching. I ain't got much to my saddlebags. A shirt to replace this one would be a kindness."

She nodded and disappeared behind a hanging cloth.

Burn took the two sacks and headed out the front door, met immediately by the brightness of the noon sun and a whicker from the bay mare. As he approached her, he became aware of two things—his arm was going to give him hell, and the two children had followed him.

The girl, Henrietta—damned fool name, best call her Missy—she reached up and patted Beauty's nose. "What's her name, mister?"

"Beauty."

Then the boy spoke: "Don't go fooling with my sister . . . she just wants to know the horse's name."

Burn laughed, then hung the two bags from the saddle horn.

"Her name is Beauty. Her papa was a friend of mine." He thought on the peculiarity of those words, but they were a kind of truth. It shut the boy up, too.

The two children eyed Burn, then very gently the girl went back to patting wherever she could reach of the mare's shiny hide.

Beauty lowered her head and rubbed her muzzle in the child's hair and the girl laughed as she played with Beauty's whiskers.

Then Ardith Robey called from the doorway, and, without looking back, both children ran to her.

Burn hesitated, then turned, and the woman was holding out a light-colored bundle. "Here," she said. "Keep them . . . they belonged to our eldest son."

CHAPTER FOUR

He rode two hours by his reckoning, followed by a beating sun that spoiled his disposition. The cheer left in him by that child's touch on Beauty's muzzle was lost to a gathering fever and throbbing pain. He knew he was in for a day or two of pure misery.

There was a hillside that went down to a small inlet of river water shaded by a big cottonwood. A small meadow spread out at the back of the tree, displaying evidence of a rich spring.

Grasses, water, shade, the river close by—the perfect setting for what was about to lay him low.

Beauty was content to be hobbled and turned loose. Burn arranged a soft bed on the river sand, hung his gear from the lowest cottonwood branch, drank a lot of clean spring water, then washed his face, hands, and neck, not having the energy to get out of his clothes despite a growing rankness from riding and the heat. He knew to keep the bandage dry.

Among the various delights, given him by Mrs. Ardith Robey, were a stew, bacon, some coffee beans, a loaf of bread, and a jar of pickles. He figured to eat the stew first, then work on the bacon, probably from their own pig, and a few cans of beans, one jar of peach preserves. If it weren't for the rising fever, he'd be in cowboy heaven. Then again, if the dog had been rabid, he'd be approaching heaven soon, or at least some place other than where he sat right now. It seemed a morbid thought to have when all this food sat in front of him, so Burn started a fire, boiled coffee, and heated up the stew in his fry pan. The smell started out sweet until he forked in a mouthful and his belly quit on him. He lay back, exhausted and sliding in and out consciousness.

He woke to birds yakking at him, and, once he got his eyes open, he saw two ravens standing in the middle of his fry pen, pecking each other, then reaching down to drag up the black and shiny remains of the burned stew. Next to the fry pan lay a glass jar on its side and he could see where gravy had soaked into the sand. There wasn't a bite left of the meal the woman had shared with him.

When he sat up, he was seeing double. Damn those four ravens setting in his fry pan! He wondered what *they* would taste like, slow roasted, but who would remove the damned feathers?

He lay down again, having decided that thinking and looking weren't worth the bother, and he went back to sleep quickly, while the ravens continued their argument.

This time he woke slowly, rubbing his jaw and feeling his whiskers, a good growth. Sitting up merely strained his tired muscles, but no head spin, no ache. He was alive, the ravens were gone, and the fry pan was pecked clean. He itched in a few places, mostly around the bandaged arm. He felt pretty good about the itch; it meant he was healing.

The river water was calm, sun sparkling off its surface, and it was simple to get quickly out of his half shirt, wool pants, and socks that were falling to pieces. Finally shucking out of his combinations, he walked into the water, wounded arm held high as he untied and unwrapped the soiled cloth.

The air felt good on the puckered skin, so he thought to hell with it and threw himself out into the current, bucking against the water's pull, going under, then pushing through and up, sputtering and smiling until he heard a whinny. Sure enough, Beauty was at the edge of the river, still hobbled, not daring to come in.

He half swam to her, standing slowly, letting the water run off him. Damn he felt good, even if hungry and weak, but damned good. He was back to the living.

Beauty stuck out her nose and Burn held up his hand. She licked his fingers, then butted him on the chest with her head and he fell into the water, laughing out loud. The poor horse tried to jump backward away from his splashing while Burn sat in the water, choking and wet and pleased with himself.

A week of riding north. It was cold up beyond Taos, most likely into Colorado now, and too cold when he got up in the mornings. His own stink was getting to him again, and even the mare shook her head and raised her upper lip, mimicking her sire when he got wind of a scent. Burn's whole body itched. Remnants of the fever, days riding chilled, then sweaty. He couldn't blame the mare when she turned her head away as he tried to bridle her.

It had to be almost winter now, pure cold, and

the trees had shed all their dried leaves. In the morning, frost covered his blankets, which made the mare hump her back when he saddled her. Still he rode north. No reason other than that's where he was headed and wouldn't quit now.

Midday, of course, he had to shuck his sheepskin and sometimes hang his hat on the saddle horn and let the warm air bathe him. It was surely a pleasure, that soft easy touch on his upturned face. The blaze of sun against his closed eyelids supplied a peace.

However, the thought of one more night of being cold to the bone needled Burn. He was tiring of frozen hard ground, and the cold wind blowing hard into every corner of his bedroll. So this night Burn dug in under a juniper, scaring out small varmints, but he didn't care, the cold had gotten to him. Even that damned dog bite had begun to ache again when he woke in the early morning.

It hurt to move. He was bent over, lamed like those old men he'd watched and made fun of long ago. He'd never be that old, not him. He walked a bit, stomping his feet, blowing on his hands, hoping for a miracle. Getting the mare saddled and packed, even shucking into the sheepskin, was a hard task slowed by soreness in his hands, jelly in both knees.

The miracle came later, when he and the mare crested a hill and looked down into the prettiest valley Burn had ever seen. Like the valley where he had trapped the wild horses, but with knee-high grass and clusters of trees and in the far distance the glitter of a spring. Pooled water ringed with saplings, a few holding onto faded gold leaves. A big old cottonwood lording over everything—biggest damned tree Burn had ever seen.

The rest of the miracle—no fences, that and the water and only small trails for varmints and deer. No cattle sign, no platters of manure and trampled grasses. No horses, either, only a few dried piles from sometime in the past. A place he might rest for a time, give the mare a vacation. She was losing weight. The grain sack was long empty, his own few stores down to a moldy slab of bacon and one airtight of peaches. The burlaps of grub doled out by a grateful Mrs. Robey were long gone. He'd gotten a meal or two out of the bread loaf even though there had been mold on the crust. Luckily he'd been lying on the burlap bag, using it as a pillow, which had saved the bread from any four legged thieves. He had one shirt that fit well, but the other two were rags now, good for keeping in his short store of clothing. A man never knew when he might be in need of another bandage. This time, though, it wasn't going to be from any damned dog bite.

Originally Burn had decided he would ride into a village, stay a day, find a job if he could, a place to winter. Now that he had found this spot, well, this was heaven, and, if he froze out here, death suited him just fine.

Taking care of Beauty came first. He curried her back, picked out her hoofs, tested the tightness of her shoes. She'd hang here until the grass got chewed down. His hands on her ribs felt bone. He wasn't worried she'd leave. So he turned her loose, free, unfettered, and she ran a few strides, then quickly settled to the good eating.

Next, out of old habit, he hung the gear, saddle, bridle, rope, and emptied saddlebags high in the branches of the old cottonwood. He walked its circle and looked up into the high branches, marveling that something could grow to such a size. It was a big one all right.

He had too many choices for the campsite—flat thick grasses for a mattress, the cottonwood for shelter, and lower saplings that could be drawn down and pulled together to make a windbreak when he needed it.

Taking time to study the land, Burn lay back with his head on the cottonwood trunk, arms locked behind his head as a pillow. When the wind blew, he could smell himself which made him wrinkle his nose.

He stood and shucked out of his clothes, kicked them into a small pile, then thought better of it, and picked them up, carrying them into the water.

God, they smelled. He walked into the water without stopping, and, although he could freeze half to death in no time, it was clean water, clear enough that he could see his toes, the grains of sand, a few critters skittering away.

First he stuck the clothes under water, splashing them around some, rubbing the hard wool pants against the softer cotton shirt. Bits of twigs, grass, small leaves, horse hair, all floated to the surface in memory of his recent travels.

Overhead a few birds chided him for his nakedness, but the cold water felt good. He sat down, hard, and laughed as he leaned forward and ducked his head, came up sputtering. My God, the water was cold on his butt and belly. Taking fists of sand, he started scrubbing, carefully around the scars, but confident because he'd had years of washing around them. Still it made him shudder to touch them—ugly raised welts, some wider than his thumb, criss-crossing his belly, thigh, and ribs stretching around to his back. One at his throat. The few on his arms and hands weren't too bad, but the one on his belly. He winced, kept scrubbing, especially under his arms and his privates. He was extra cautious around the dog bite. It still itched, but there was a small pocket of red under one of the stitches. He needed to dig it out, but not now, not while he was enjoying himself.

When he stood, a bird shrieked and several flew

up from reeds across from the cottonwood. Burn shook his head, felt water fly off his hair, his beard, and thought he might take the time now to heat some water and shave, maybe even take a knife to his hair. Too much gray in it. He could see the silver strands pass his eyes. It had been almost black just a few years ago.

The sun was hot enough to dry him. He stood naked, allowing air and sun and the world to see his wounds. The mare raised her head and whinnied at him, birds settled in the nearby trees, and Burn let out a sigh that turned into a belch. He grinned, wiped at his damp hair, and for once felt a well-being. No gut ache, no fretting. Gone with the place where his dreams had died.

CHAPTER FIVE

Ruthie Heber knew what men looked like. She had two older brothers still at home—three had moved away. Ruthie was the baby girl, at least that's what her ma called her even though she was twelve and could take care of herself. In addition to her brothers, her ma had a new man that didn't button up when he needed to, like he was advertising something no other man had. Ruthie knew this latest man, Cal, wouldn't be staying long. While Ma liked her men, she didn't take to rudeness or such displays as Cal was offering up to the family. This one, down by the cottonwood, though . . . he was ugly and skinny and too short, and, when he took off those torn clothes, he got uglier.

But the mare that the mister down there rode, she was a beauty. Good legs and a fine head, an eye able to see and know the world around her. She was a rich dark red color with that black mane and tail—Ruthie liked the colors together. She herself had nothing to ride but a speckled Appaloosa, with white around his eye and striped feet, and even his thing was speckled. This mare, though, she was sleek and pretty to watch, and Ruthie thought she would like to ride a mare like her. It would be something special to sit up there and have the world see her and know that she, Ruthie Heber, knew a good horse and deserved to ride one.

The man was bent over searching through a bedroll by Ruthie's reckoning, and she got so embarrassed that she slid back down the hill to her old roan Appaloosa that was chewing at grass and half sleeping. She startled the roan and he raised his head and started to whicker. Ruthie grabbed his nose. She didn't want any sound telling that scrawny naked man he was being watched.

She jumped for the stirrup and found it with the wrong foot, so she pulled herself up, and then switched feet and threw the other leg over the battered old-time saddle. The roan was used to her peculiar way of mounting. He was a tall skinny bronco and it wasn't easy for Ruthie to get on. Another thing she liked about the bay mare down by the pond was that she wasn't as big as this monster horse. And she sure was a whole lot prettier.

Ruthie had been coming everyday for a week now. She had made herself a soft place nestled near a rock, where she could lie flat and then raise her head, peer over the rim, and watch him. He didn't do much usually, just laid around. He seemed to sleep a lot in the beginning. He spent time neatening up his camp. Once she caught him out in the middle of the pond, his skin-white rump pushed out of the water, his head up, his hands grabbing something and pulling him forward. He didn't sink, he didn't fight, he scooped and kicked and made his way across the pond and back. She wanted someone to teach her how to do that.

Sometimes he caught up the bay mare that always nuzzled him, and he would cup her nose and seem to talk into her ear as the two of them stood side by side. Ruthie'd never seen a man talk to a horse like that. She wondered if the horse talked back.

His nakedness scared her even as she was curious. There had been glimpses before, and she'd quickly run away or cover her eyes. But he had to get naked, she guessed, when he went in the water to do that wind-milling around. She had asked her ma what you called that wind-milling, and she had said it was swimming, and then wanted to know why Ruthie had asked. She had had to make up a lie quickly. "'Cause I want to learn how to paddle in the water when it's hot and I figured there was a word for what I couldn't do." That had seemed to satisfy her ma, who knew, once Ruthie got started, it could be tough getting her to shut down with the talking. It was useful, knowing this much about yourself.

He was a skinny thing, and scarred—most of them were old, faded, white like his skin, but ridged and raised up so she couldn't help but see them. Except there was a red wound on his left arm, above the elbow, that he sometimes rubbed at, never quite touching the wound itself. It had to be recent, she thought.

Then one day she witnessed him take a knife, burn its tip in a low fire, and dig into the wound. He seemed to be picking out small things that flew through the air. Then she heard him groan as blood dripped out. But he was quiet as he laid the heated knife tip on the bleeding. It made her sick to her stomach, and she had to lead her Roany, which is what she called her horse, for a few minutes before she felt steady enough to climb up into the saddle. The man might be a scrawny thing, but he had courage, she'd give him that.

Cal, Ma's man, had got himself a splinter stuck under a fingernail once, a ratty little bit of wood, and, by the Lord above—she'd heard her Ma say that once—you'd've thought Cal had been scalped. Ma had pulled the darned thing out, and Cal held his hand like it was broken. Ma had shoved him outside, telling him to get away till he could act like a man. That, too, had let Ruthie know Cal wasn't long in their life.

Sometimes her mister, as she now thought of the man with the mare, would take out a brush he had stuffed into a pair of saddlebags that looked as old as forever, but soft, loose as if they had been oiled and taken care of. Not like the way her brothers left things lying on the ground where she fell over them, or hung somewhere until they got covered in dusty webs and made her sneeze when she pushed by them. Harness bridles with those blinkers, and that heavy old collar, the wooden shaped sticks she'd heard called hames—they were all rotting because the boys didn't care.

Her mister, he'd take that brush to the mare, one hand following the brush's path, probably feeling for bumps and cuts Ruthie decided. He sure could make that pretty mare shine, and, when he was done, putting the brush away after scraping it on his boot so dust would fly up, the mare would nuzzle against him. Sometimes he'd lean on her, the two of them motionless, bound together.

He was funny to watch, whistling, even fishing out of the pond. He didn't catch much, but she took note of a few rabbit skins hung out to dry. She figured the man was just making do.

Then one day that no-good Cal left the pen gate open and Lady, the brindle cow, disappeared. Her calf had been partially weaned and was in a separate pen, so the family could share in the milk. Ruthie liked the cheese Ma made, and the taste of fresh butter on the bread pulled from the bake oven to the back of the old fireplace. The plan was to slaughter the calf soon for the winter.

Well, her ma was so mad when the cow escaped that Ruthie was happy to go looking for it, even if she couldn't go and see her mister. Her ma was fearful Lady had gotten onto Haydock Carpenter's land and that they'd have to fight for her return. Old man Carpenter was cranky; even Ruthie knew that from her ma's talking. That was probably why Ma was so mad, thinking about having to deal with the old man and that new wife of his.

So Ruthie saddled Roany, and climbed onto the saddle. She checked the yard first. There were tracks around the side of the barn, where they kept the bull calf in an open stall. She found some dirt dug up, a middle rail from the pen shoved free, but no mama cow around.

A few tracks went up over the rise, wandered

sideways some, and then made a straight line toward Carpenters' place. Ruthie kicked the roan, and he threw up his head and sort of stumbled into a slow jog. Not fast enough to catch Lady, but the best she could get out of Roany. It was only her imagination, but she could almost feel the smooth trot, the easy lope of the bay mare back at the pond. It would be like riding the best horse ever in the world; she could tell from the mare's eye and the way her mister cared for her.

CHAPTER SIX

Burn woke to a peaceful, almost warm morning, no frost, no wind, a real pleasure. He had the coffee boiling quickly, and he sat back to enjoy a quiet moment. The mare was lying down, knees folded beneath her belly, nose resting on the ground, as peaceful as the morning itself. Then he noticed a deer entering at the far edge of the pond, alert but not yet aware of Burn or the mare. Burn set his cup down, stood slowly, and reached for his rifle. He had his fingers on the chilled metal when the deer raised its head, perhaps having seen him grab the rifle, and bounded off through the high grass.

The mare woke at the deer's escape. Burn stumbled in his hurry to shoot and the mare came up from her sleep into a panic. She spun around and kicked out, then took off, tail high over her back, kicking, feeling good again. She was a joy to watch until Burn realized the mare was leaving their small valley.

Burn's hand folded over the rifle stock, pulled it to him, and swung it around to fire. The damned deer was gone, and so was the mare. He rested the rifle butt on the ground, wiped his face, and felt a complete fool. From peace to nothing in maybe two minutes.

He walked maybe a half hour before finding the mare. She was pulling at stalky grass, and barely turned her head at his approach. When he got too close, she moved away, not bothering to raise her head from the grass. When she stopped so quickly, Burn knew what was wrong. Holding out his hand, palm up, fingers wiggling, he crooned to the mare and moved in closer. This time she raised her head and he watched her eye real closely. She took one step and that placid dark eye suddenly showed white. Burn tried to reach her, but she leaned away and shook one front leg. He heard the sound, and called to her over the pounding in his throat, his head—good God damn.

The wire snaked up through the tan grasses and thin soil as the mare set back and pulled, the front leg drawn away from her, haunches set close to the ground. Her other front hoof dug in, but nothing gave except the band of hide around her cannon bone. He saw the blood, could taste it in his mouth, and he spat to the side.

"Hey, Beauty . . . it's me. It's OK, girl. Settle down. I'll take care of you. Won't hurt none at all." He was lying, but any words would do.

She quit pulling, that one leg stretched out, her body weight leaning on the tender skin. Burn wanted to throw up, but he stepped to her shoulder. She tried to hop away from him, but the pain stopped her. She shook, whickered, dug in with her hind legs, and then fell to her side, leg bleeding badly now, damp and hot where Burn grabbed hide and bone above the wire and tried to touch the mare's neck. She threw him off, so he sat on her, on the flat of her jowl, and she trembled under him but had to be still.

He had nothing, no knife or wire cutters, no rope, bridle—nothing. Anything that might be useful was back at camp. He shucked out of his shirt and tore it, wrapped his hands, and bent the wire back, pulling hide with it, but there was no other way. The mare screamed under Burn as he fought to keep her head down as her hindquarters rose, her legs kicked out.

He got it, bending and spreading the wire, so he could open a hole and slide the mare's leg out. It caught for a moment on the rise of the hoof near the coronet band and left a pinprick of blood as it scraped down the horn, leaving a white line. The wire band slipped free, and Burn's hands held only the bleeding leg. He quickly unwrapped his shirt padding and tied one sleeve across the wound, another one above it, and then tore strips from the body of the shirt and knotted them before slipping them around the mare's neck. He felt her skin shudder against his touch.

It was rough, but he stood quickly and stepped back while the mare struggled, got her legs under her, and tossed her head and neck, bringing herself up to a sitting position before standing. When she shook to free herself of the sand, the injured leg buckled. She grunted, went down in front, and came up to strike out at Burn.

He tugged on the noose around her neck, and she looked at him, ears pinned back. "Beauty, it's all right now." At his voice, her ears went forward and she pushed out her muzzle, touching his bare arm.

At first Beauty walked fine on the leg, and that gave Burn hope. By the time they reached camp, the blood had stopped and it looked like, maybe, the cut was not much more than a bad scratch.

Burn was shivering, conscious of his own white skin with those angry scars across his belly. Even the one on his arm, that damned dog bite, seemed raw and open, and there was pain in his gut again. He found another shirt, one that Ardith Robey had given him to ease her conscience. He put it on, buttoned a few buttons, and then bridled the mare, led her to the pond, but she wouldn't walk in with him. He had figured that might be, so he slipped up on her back and rode her in a small circle, then into the cold water. Her whole body shuddered again, splashing up cold drops that chilled Burn, but she was standing in over her knees and he made her stand there for what felt like forever.

When he let her come out, she was shaking. So was he. Burn slipped down, untied the drenched cotton bandage, and saw pink flesh over white bone, clean flesh, bloodless now, no pumping, no red flow. It was bad, though, worse than he had thought. Bone showed through hide, no cut tendons, but close. He shuddered, stood up slowly, and touched Beauty's neck to hide his own fear. He wrapped the leg again, glad he'd kept those shirt pieces.

He couldn't hobble her, so, with a pounding heart, he turned her loose. She took one bobbing step, stopped, put her head down, and closed her eyes. She was exhausted. He was, too.

Burn spent the next four days working on the leg. He had the mare stand in the small pond, until he thought his own feet would turn blue. He spent hours pulling grass for her, making sure she had enough to eat, and, when she did try to graze, he tied her so she wouldn't tear open the wound.

It came to him too frequently that without the

mare he was lost, alone in country he didn't know. Tracks led in many directions, but he knew one trail could lead a half mile to a house while another could lead thirty miles to nothing. The mare's leg quit bleeding through the tight wrap of his torn shirt, but Burn didn't like the heat under his fingers when he gently, barely touched the broken skin.

Without her, he was a dead man—a death of little consequence, except perhaps to himself. He imagined himself a pile of whitened bones, maybe tripped over by a kid going down to fish, knocked apart, and carried off until a single bone, resting in a mound of sand, meant nothing to those passing through.

A half hour by the sun, on Ruthie's first attempt to try to find Lady, and she was home, telling Ma that, no, she hadn't seen the brindle cow. She'd followed the tracks to a creekbed but couldn't figure out which tracks, coming out, belonged to their cow. Tracks didn't have color, she told her ma. The tracks of a single cow, even one with the strange markings that Lady had—a white face and those funny stripes running through her tan hide—weren't any easier to read. She'd go out again later, Ruthie said, maybe try to the west or up against Mr. Carpenter's fence line. The boys sometimes cut that fence and didn't mend it properly; a cow might get in by mistake.

Ma seemed angry at Ruthie's report, so she went out and tended to the roan Appaloosa, and fed hay to the lonesome bull calf. She tried to remember exactly what she'd said that could have made her ma so riled. Probably had to do with that Cal still hanging around.

Days later Ruthie still hadn't found the cow, so she went into the cabin and straight to her mama, leaning against her warmth, distressed that she'd been useless in the hunt. Out in back, she could hear the bull calf bellowing for his mouthful of warm milk.

The mother touched the top of her daughter's head, not really thinking about the child but wanting instinctively to reassure her. "You'll find her. We need that milk for her calf. He's still penned up, ain't he?" Her worn fingers felt the child's head nod vigorously, up and down—silence being Ruthie's preferred method of communication until she got on a talking streak, and then it was nothing but noise and thoughts and words all caught up in each other.

Margaret Lewis Heber—actually there were more names to go with the husbands but she had given up after a while and had stuck with Ruthie's father's name, finding it easier that way on the children. It wasn't that she was particular or fickle, it was that the men had died, or walked away, gone hunting with a friend and never had come back. Margaret didn't bother with a divorce when these disappearances occurred; she just moved to another place where there would always be another man.

This one—Cal—was about to go. He was pretty enough—tall and strong, taller than her, just the way she liked them. Also handsome in a smooth, slick manner, with thick blond hair and light blue eyes. She didn't always want to look into those eyes, in which meanness showed sometimes. And recently he had been acting irresponsible around Ruthie, who, at twelve, had no figure yet and had her older brothers' bad mouth at times, but, still, she was a girl and Cal needed to mind his manners. And it was Cal who had turned out the cow without her calf and yet couldn't be bothered to go hunting for it. So Margaret—Maggie was what everyone called her—had had to send out a child to deal with the problem resulting from his laziness. Damn the man, and she would tell him so to his face as soon as he showed up at her cabin. *Her* cabin. She'd remind him of that fact, see what came up into those hard blue eyes.

Of course, Ruthie could track and ride better than most men, and, if the child said the cow went through Carpenter's cut fence, then it was true, and there would be trouble. Carpenter wasn't bad, but his wife was a harridan who doubted Maggie's marriage stories and spoke to the folks in the towns of Bayfield and Durango as if Maggie were a whore and not a properly married woman.

Maggie moved her hand from Ruthie's head to her shoulder and felt the thinness of bone in the child. It marveled her that this little thing, with no male muscle and no female body yet, could have such a mouth and such courage.

"You want some switchell, Ruthie? I made up a new batch even though it's coming winter. You doing chores, and the boys, too . . . well, I thought you might like the switchell." It was an old recipe from her mother's folks, out of Vermont they were. Water and cider vinegar and some molasses, a handful of oatmeal. Made for a head-clearing drink on a hot day, and some folks, mostly children like Ruthie, would chew the oatmeal set up with the molasses like a sweet.

She got the child settled in a chair and was holding a glass in one hand, reaching for the pitcher, when Cal stomped through the door, scaring both of them. Maggie's hand missed in grabbing for the pitcher, bumping it instead and causing it to rock on the table. She almost caught it, but didn't, only felt its slick surface as it tilted, and then poured out the amber liquid, splashing all over Cal's boots and jeans.

Ruthie caught the pitcher before it fell, and there was a moment's suspicion in Maggie that her daughter had figured out just when she could save the pitcher and still get Cal wet. It was how Ruthie's mind worked, quickly, so quickly so that she didn't think about the consequences of her actions.

Cal slapped Ruthie, sending the child reeling. The pitcher broke against the stone fireplace, sending crystal pieces all over the girl and the floor. Maggie went to her daughter, holding her down, and all the while yelling at Cal to get out, get out of their house, how dare he hurt a child, how dare he slap her Ruthie. Cal stood in the doorway, frowning.

One hand on her daughter's back, Maggie realized the child was crying, something Ruthie rarely did. If she was cut or hurt, oh, Lordy, that man would feel the edge of a fry pan or a stick of wood. Ruthie rolled over, mindful of her mother picking out glass from her hair, her shirt, on the floor where she had fallen.

"It's all right, Ma. I ain't cut. He just scared me is all."

Ever true Ruthie, looking out for her mama, instead of worrying about herself. Maggie kissed the child's hair above her closed eyes, and tasted the sharp prick of the smallest sliver of glass on her lip. She picked Ruthie up, plucking at her clothes, seeing all those shiny bits sticking in her shirt.

She brushed through Ruthie's hair, paying no attention to Cal's blaming and mumbling. A man that had no better sense than to hit a child deserved a lot more than Cal was getting from Maggie's mouth. She intended to let the son-of-a . . . well, she never said those things out loud, even if she thought them too often. She could be too hot-tempered just like her first husband had said—hot-tempered the way he had liked her and taken her to him, laughing as she struggled and swore.

Now he was gone, the best of the lot. He'd been taken by a fever that had sickened her three oldest boys, too, but they had been young and had survived. Their pa hadn't made it. Then there was the youngest boy's pa, and he'd sired Ruthie, too, which was why she had kept his name. She'd never bothered to tell Tad his father was someone else. It would be too confusing, so no need to bother. They were all her children, every one of them.

She helped Ruthie out of her shirt, saying: "Careful now." Then she handed her the shirt. "Don't shake it. Wait till you get outside . . . but don't go near the pens."

Then Maggie looked for Cal, but he, too, was gone, and about time. *Good,* she thought, *no need to bother with him any more.* About all that he had offered Maggie was that he was good in the bed, and she appreciated a man who knew what he was doing, but that was all he could do well and it wasn't enough to keep him around. She had children to raise, and Cal only got in the way.

The sound of retreating hoof beats sounded purely good to Maggie. She glanced through the door and saw the back end of Cal's fine horse headed west. *Best place for them,* she thought, although she had to admit she would miss the occasional opportunity she had had to ride his horse. Now all they had was the roan Appaloosa Ruthie said belonged only to her.

Maggie called out for Ruthie, and jumped when the child spoke almost at her elbow.

"Glad the son-of-a-bitch's gone."

"Ruthie!" Maggie had to act tough with the girl, but the child was right; they were both glad Cal was gone. "You don't say such things."

"Ah, Ma, you know it's the truth."

Maggie knelt down to face her daughter and patted the brushed strands of her brown hair. Then her fingers combed through the thickness, finding no more glass shards to prick her skin. When she heard another commotion outside the door, Maggie looked up in time to see the brindle cow lumber across the yard, her huge udder slapping from side to side, milk being squeezed out by her hind legs.

Ruthie heard the bull calf's bellow and she pushed away from her mama, knowing it was her responsibility to take care of the family cow.

The bossy cow wouldn't let the boys touch her; their hands were just too rough. Lady would stick out her head and bellow whenever they tugged at her teats and made their crude jokes. So it fell to Ruthie to do the milking, resting her head against Lady's warm flank, sitting on the end of her stained tail, talking to the miserable cow as she pulled and pulled. The bucket was full by the time the bull calf started bellowing for some of that sweet foamy milk.

The next day, Maggie let Ruthie go off on her own without comment. She rode west, then slightly south, not having to look for Lady, wanting to see her mister and the pretty mare.

This time she stayed on Roany as she peered down in the valley. There he was, her mister, sitting on the mare, who was limping as she came out of the water. On land, the man slid down off the mare's shiny back. He wore boots and pants, but his shirt was barely buttoned, and, across his belly, those scars flashed at Ruthie, raised and angry, and they made her stomach queasy again.

She forgot she was spying, and yelled at him: "Hey, mister, what'd you do to that pretty mare?"

On his knees, Burn froze, his hands clenching the mare's leg. Beauty reached down, nipped at his shoulder. Burn let go, stood slowly, holding hard to the bridle reins, uncertain and surprised.

The voice hollered again, something Burn couldn't make out. Then a small nubbin on a lanky red Appaloosa came sliding down the hill. The child, he thought it was a girl, stopped the tall horse so quickly she almost bounced out of the saddle. When the mare kicked out and fell to her knees, the Appaloosa slid sideways and lost his rider. Only Burn remained still, bridle reins held so loosely in his hand that they pulled through until, at the last moment, he remembered and closed his fist, holding up the mare's head. She stood next to him, shaken almost as badly as he was.

The red roan trotted to the mare. They touched noses, whickered at each other, and, when the mare rubbed her head on Burn's arm, the roan settled.

It came to Burn that the rider was slow to move, so he let go of the mare, who stayed with the roan as he walked up the sandy hill. The child was sitting up now, blowing dirt from her mouth, and rubbing the side of her head, but Burn didn't see any blood, so he figured she hadn't been hurt too badly.

"What's wrong with the mare?" she asked again.

Burn shook his head, opened his mouth, and thought better of it. Instead, Burn grinned, wiped his face, then felt the swing of his shirt tails, and remembered he was half dressed, and in front of a girl child. He quickly turned his back, buttoned up, and tucked in his shirt before turning around again.

" 'S all right, mister. I been watching you is all. Even seen you get out into the water and not drown. How'd you do that? I tried and went under, and my older brother . . . he had to come get me."

She sure could talk, Burn thought to himself,

and. . . . She'd watched him in the water! Burn blushed, feeling the heat flush his whole body as he walked back to the grazing horses. They were nose to nose, seeking out the best blades and snipping gently. Occasionally the bay mare would rub against the roan's leg or shoulder and the taller horse would brace himself, nickering softly and arching his neck.

That child had seen him naked. It was wrong. She was a child, but to hell with her. It sounded to Burn as though she'd been watching him on several occasions and that told him how badly he was slipping, losing the abilities needed to survive. Another instinct he had lost, gone from his younger self, which annoyed him more than knowing a child had seen him naked. It even frightened him a little. This knowledge about himself confirmed what age and sitting on a front porch had done to his life.

He caught up her horse, had to drag it, but finally the roan followed him, and the bay mare came limping along. He needed a new bandage for the wound, and some sulphur tar, anything to keep out infection. At least now he had a chance to find a home nearby. The child owed him that much for her spying.

"Girl, you live close?"

She took the reins to her horse, fished out something from her mouth, and tried standing. " 'Bout a half hour's ride."

"How long leading a sore mare? And while it ain't none of your business . . . she got herself caught in some god-damn' wire." He couldn't stop the cursing, didn't want to. Damned wire always got him so mad.

She glared at him. "I ain't taking you home with me."

"You got no choice. I may be slow, but I can follow your tracks. Don't matter how far out you ride to confuse me, I'll find your home. The mare needs more tending and medicines than I got on me."

That spooked her. Those shiny blue eyes got wet, and the girl took one step toward the mare. "She's right pretty. You think I could ride her?"

"Not on that leg. Nothing rides her till she heals. You got salve and bandages to your house?"

The child got mad, and Burn might have grinned but he knew well enough that it would hurt her pride.

"My ma can take care of 'most anything, mister," Ruthie said, looking somewhat defensive. Then: "How'd she get cut again? I was more mad than listening."

This conversation was getting peculiar for Burn, talking to this bit of a thing as if they were equals. His hands twitched, his mouth got tight, and he looked away from the girl. "Wire."

She came back: "That what cut you up, mister?"

89

He turned to look at her, and she pulled back a step, saying: "I was just asking."

He packed up the bedroll, his rank sheepskin coat, fry pan, and coffee pot, stuffing everything randomly into the saddlebags. The saddle and blankets went on the mare, then he tied everything to its strings, prompting the girl to question him again.

"You said she wasn't going to be ridden . . . what's that saddle weigh? More'n me I bet."

"The saddle stays quiet on her, you'll wiggle 'round and throw her off balance. Besides, I can't leave my stuff here, unless you think that App you're riding'll carry the saddle and my gear."

She dismissed the suggestion without bothering to answer, saying: "Well, you ain't staying at our house."

"I'm trading your family some chores for some bandages and salve."

The girl came right back at him, face turning red around her freckles. "She ain't gonna like it."

Burn studied the child, saying what he was thinking out loud, and surprising them both. "Your ma's anything like you, child, she'll take pity on the mare. No one with a heart wants such a beautiful thing to suffer."

He finished tying the last string, patted the mare's neck, and wished he'd shaved and groomed this morning before he'd gotten himself into this mess. Watching the kid try to climb on the ugly roan almost prompted him to offer help, but he'd learned this much already—stay out of the way of anything having to do with pride, and she was prideful for such a scrawny thing.

He shook his head and bent down to rearrange the sleeve of his shirt on the mare's leg. He didn't want dirt and such getting into the open wound while traveling. This kid, he thought again to himself, barely a grown child, had seen him naked. Since he'd been a baby, there were only two people that had known him that way: the Hildahls—Katherine, while nursing him back to health, and Davey, who had helped her. The few women, well . . . his face caught on fire again. Burn had never been much with the ladies, even in his youth. He couldn't bear the questions, the talking too much, when all he wanted was what they were selling.

He thought about letting the kid ride out, and just staying at the pond and the cottonwood and the good grass. He could work on the mare himself until the leg healed. He was finding it hard to look in the girl's eyes, knowing she'd seen more of him than anyone was meant to. He could feel each scar throb, and the new one itched, and it was wrong to know what she knew.

It wasn't right, but for now he had no choice. There was heat in the mare's leg and he had nothing in those damned saddlebags to treat such a vicious wound. He had left his old life in a hurry, forgetting to bring along some of the necessities. He could visualize the tin of salve back at the cabin, a stinking tar that took care of many problems. Buried now, along with the shelf it sat on, under the weight of the torn-down roof, the destroyed corral poles. Still it wasn't right, what the girl had seen.

It took more than an hour to get wherever they were headed. Burn walked, cursing his heeled boots, but not wanting to ask the girl for a lift. Besides, the hindquarters to that old roan didn't look too comfortable—a high bony spine and sloping croup. Walking was the better choice, but he stopped frequently, telling the girl he was letting the mare rest. It was the truth. The leg did hurt Beauty now. He could see it. She'd hold it off the ground, and, when he touched her foreleg, she flinched, which meant fluid was swelling up the tissues.

He damned the wire, damned the fool that had pulled down a fence and left coils scattered and hidden in the grasses to bring down a good mare. He might as well damn the entire world for the unfeeling act of a fool. Too many folks were that way, not considerate about who else might have to walk along the path they had used.

By the time they started on a well-trod track with other narrowed tracks slicing in at angles, Burn was footsore and the mare limping badly.

The girl wanted them both to hurry. He told the girl to go ahead, and she kicked at the Appaloosa gelding but the ugly roan had no intention of leaving the mare, so the lamed group struggled up a hill slowly, before a small cabin appeared.

The cabin was well built and sturdy, with a good-size barn, and corrals at the back. A calf bellowed and the Appaloosa gelding raised his head, whinnied a high-pitched, foolish response.

CHAPTER SEVEN

His given name was Haydock Carpenter. At times, his wife, new to him still, took pleasure from calling him Doc, as if that were his profession. Particularly when they were bedding each other. Women weren't supposed to like those things, but she surely gave him pleasure in their times, and, by God, it was an improvement on his first and second wives, who had babies willingly enough, but didn't seem to like the process of creating them.

This old gal, Rose, she was good in some ways and terrible in others, a real whirlwind to live with. She couldn't cook and she kept after him to make the ranch bigger—big enough to take in the whole damned country. He thought the land he owned now, the sections and grants and rights, was more than any one man could use, especially now that towns were growing and cattle being shipped by rail cars close by, and there wasn't any open range.

She wanted a fancy new house built in town, and a smaller one out by the pond in Salt Valley. Haydock was inclined to neither venture. It meant spending money on something they didn't need. He already had a good house, with a stone fireplace and windows looking out to the distance that she didn't have to wash, no, sir. He had the ranch women do that job, along with many of the other chores. These women lived with their husbands in the old adobes their parents had built, comfortable with work on the Rafter JX and keeping to the way of life they preferred.

Haydock Carpenter, he wasn't so much in love with the woman to want to please her that way. He'd keep what was his, making sure no man took from him, but he didn't want more. All his children had died, none of them reaching more than a few years of life. He grieved still, knowing it was no longer possible to have a family. Not with this woman. Besides, he wouldn't wish her as a mama to any babe of his. Still she pleased him in bed and was a face smiling back at him, most of the time.

He went outside, carrying a tin cup of the thick coffee he liked and she didn't. She preferred to have him sit at a table and use fancy cups with saucers. He accommodated her most of the time, but this morning he wanted peace and quiet and no fool woman serving him. He'd always been his own keeper, almost seventy-five years now, even when growing up and living with his mother and then later with his previous wives. He took care of himself, didn't plan to let this one change a lifelong habit.

The sun was up behind him, glancing light onto the hills to the west. Dark shadows moved down and then up as the light grew. He'd had news almost a week now, news he didn't like. Those Heber boys had cut his fence again, and this time their milch cow had gotten into his good alfalfa. What those fool boys couldn't be made to understand was that it wasn't safe for the cow, but neither seemed to understand or care. She'd die from the gas in a while—frozen alfalfa turned to poison and they had had a frost two nights ago. He'd sent a hand to chouse out the cow, but the boy had come back, saying the tracks showed the cow had gone back through the fence on her own. He'd put the fence back together. "Was that enough, *señor*?"

Haydock had grinned at the boy's cleverness and told him that most milch cows had their own secret ways, and, if the fence was mended, nothing else needed doing.

The more troubling news had come from Raul Garcia, a tough hand, but loyal, and Haydock had no reason to doubt him. Some ranny had set himself up with a camp inside Salt Valley and that had stirred Haydock. A day or two was one thing, but Raul said he'd checked back, and the man was still there.

Haydock drained the rest of the coffee, tipped the cup over, and watched the sludge of fine grounds slide out, drip onto the grass. The lawn she called it, a fancied-up term for grass. And, by God and dammit, Haydock wasn't having no lawn to his ranch house getting in the way of him dumping out coffee grounds.

He decided he'd ride over to the Heber place, speak to that woman again about her boys. She was a pretty thing, tall and lean with a good shape under those loose-fitting dresses and dark hair that made a man think of other things while he was looking into those blue eyes. She tried keeping herself plain, but it wasn't any use. She was a looker all right.

One advantage that came with being the boss was that as he lazed along toward the corral, Rogelio caught sight of him and came bursting out of the cook shack, wiping breakfast off his face and nodding. Rogelio had been with him from the beginning.

"Which horse you want today, *Señor* Carpenter?"

Haydock liked this small show of respect, of knowing who he was.

"The black colt," he said. "He's been good

enough since we cut him, and it ain't a far piece I'm riding. . . ." He added: "Thanks, Rogelio. You roping out that son'll make the day go easy for me." He'd learned to say that word thanks more lately. Of course, *gracias* would be more popular with most of his hands, but he always thought of it too late. He didn't speak Spanish, but at least he was learning manners in his old age.

Carpenter was a tall man with the years underlined by the seams in his face, a belly hanging over his belt. His hands were mottled. Two of the fingers were missing tips and he walked half sideways from a badly set leg. Getting on the black colt was difficult for him, and Rogelio had to hold the young colt while Haydock struggled with the stirrup and pushed off, grabbing hard to the horn. It used to be he could mount up without even thinking about it, but those days were gone, like most of his hair.

Only his eyes showed the man fully; hazel eyes ringed with a darker green, vivid eyes with a slow growing film that dimmed their color. He had a reputation as a man who knew how to size up man or beast, land, a situation, with just a quick assessment. But those day were few and far between now, for Carpenter was having trouble with his vision. He could see shapes and sizes, but not features, and distance confused him. Bright light made distinguishing things even harder. The doctor in Denver had told him he was suffering from cataracts, but they weren't bad yet. He hated the thought of what the future would be like if this was just the beginning.

It usually took him two tries to judge the distance between his boot and the oxbow stirrup. It made him mad enough to curse, but he could count on Rogelio to remain quiet about the problems he was having. The man was nearly as old as Haydock.

Settled in the old Frazier he'd ridden for thirty years, Haydock felt a feathery touch on his leg.

"You be careful, *señor*, this colt is still not to be trusted," Rogelio cautioned.

Two old men, who both knew the truth about aging but wouldn't let on to those younger. Rogelio would not speak of the coming blindness, but he had seen the signs. Once, recently, he had come up to Haydock and said quietly that when one becomes older, "as you and I have, parts of the body give up long before the spirit." Carpenter had nodded at the truth, and they had never spoken of it again.

Until now, when Rogelio was subtly questioning his boss' choice of mounts. Haydock had a reason for wanting the black saddled: he wanted to ride in on the prancing colt and impress the pretty lady, Maggie Heber. An old man's vanity, yes, but worth the risk, with so little joy left in life except for bedding his new wife, and riding a good horse.

Hell, he thought, *I'll get tossed on my head, and the wife and the horses'll never notice the difference.* He nodded down to Rogelio and reined the black towards the west, and then somewhat south.

At first he snugged up on the reins and that kept the black to an uneasy jog. Haydock stood in the stirrups with one hand coiled under the saddle swell above the horse's withers. The damned trot felt like it was jarring his teeth loose and it made his vision swim. *That's right,* he thought to himself, *blame the horse. It's easier than accepting the results of a long hard life, and now old age.*

Finally he gave up and let the son-of-a-bitch run. Speed couldn't undo what was happening to him, but it felt good, like living again, and the colt didn't mind the shallow ditches or deep gullies. He bellied down and jumped, and Haydock got rocketed around, but the high cantle saved him and he even pulled leather once or twice since no one was looking.

Eventually the colt tired and Haydock drew him to a walk in time to take a few deep gulps of air and wipe sweat and dust from his face. It wouldn't do to ride in damp and dirty to visit with that Heber woman.

He came over the slight rise where the cabin was set at the edge of a shallow bowl. Good cabin. Her last husband had built it some years past for his first wife. He'd died; the wife herself was long gone. Mrs. Heber had right of title by the act of establishing her home there and so far no one had come forward to challenge her.

Mrs. Rose Carpenter watched her husband and that old Mexican chew over the black colt as Haydock's boot slipped from the stirrup. He got it with a second try. *Damned old fool showing off again. Any excuse to ride over to that woman's cabin and prance himself around on a fancy-stepping horse, thinking that he's still a young man.*

As a husband he was moderate to good enough; decent to her when she demanded things and not too active in bed, wanting her to do most of the work and then tell him how great he was. She was familiar with this behavior, had been paid for her acting skills more than anything else in her life. A woman with few morals could make a good living on such lies.

Thirty-five had been the age—when she had hit that number it had all gone to hell. A stronger corset, heavy stockings to hide the veins, more powder, a darker rinse in her hair. The lies had made no difference. The men had turned to younger women, and all her efforts, her touches, and teasing hadn't returned them to her.

Her mother had named her Mabel, but, later, she had become Rose, thinking it a better choice.

When Haydock Carpenter had asked her to marry, she was glad for the chance, and she kept her name, Rose. She felt it suited her now, with her yellow hair and fleshy mouth, her extra flesh that she let slide inside a softer girdling, and her stubby legs rooted to the ground by sensible shoes. No more wearing those fancy heeled boots that killed her back, no more cinching up her loosening figure. She only had to be with the old man who didn't care she was getting fat. He liked grabbing her belly and pulling her down on him. He liked holding his woman, so he told her, and she wanted to believe him. It was easier than smiling at the boys and pushing herself on them when they wanted younger flesh and she just wanted another helping of potatoes.

This time when Haydock rode off, looking high and mighty, she stayed at the house, and worried. It wasn't just that he had married her; it was that she was getting used to the old coot.

And the old man liked what she said, most of the time, so she was beginning to find that she wanted him around. She certainly hoped he wasn't riding off to that woman's cabin, to talk about that stupid cow or spend time with the children. He couldn't have children, not with her, not with all the times she'd had the pox and kept on working. Nothing inside her was right. She couldn't bear his child even if she was young enough and he wanted to try again. He'd told her that much in his short speech about what marriage would be between them. He didn't want another family, just wanted a woman in his bed.

Tad Heber smacked his younger brother, hard, across the back of the head, then yelped and sucked on his bent finger. Tad was seventeen, dark like his mother, where Jonas was blond, more like someone that nobody but Tad remembered. Jonas hadn't known his pa that well. The man had died when thrown from a horse before Ruthie was born.

Earlier today, Tad and Jonas had gone hunting pronghorn, and they hadn't had any luck, missing every one. It didn't matter how closely or quietly they stalked, or how well they'd hidden, keeping upwind and doing what they'd been taught; the pronghorn caught their scent and bolted. And now both boys were hungry.

Jonas was acting the fool again, doing a war dance and raising his rifle like it was a spear. Tad didn't want to be shot by his own brother, so he slapped Jonas. Jonas abruptly stopped and looked at Tad like he'd committed some terrible crime.

Tad reminded Jonas that they hadn't been able to shoot one damned animal. It meant they had to tell Ma that truth, which meant she wouldn't be happy. So they walked, rifles getting too heavy to carry. One of the things that annoyed Jonas was that Ruthie had the luxury of a horse while he and Tad had to hike their way around the land.

The boys came to the house from the south and east, walking slowly, just about ready to drag the rifles, butt-end down, but not giving in to the urge, knowing it was wrong and one of them might shoot the other. Sometimes they threatened to, but they knew the importance of kin, even if they didn't share a father. Their mother thought the boys didn't know, but they weren't dumb. They could see the differences, and they knew their mother and her liking of men well enough that it made sense.

Two visitors arriving at their cabin at the same time! It was more people than had come to their cabin over the last three months. One of them was a stranger, walking with her daughter, which concerned Maggie more than the arrival of Haydock Carpenter, riding in too fast on a fancy black horse. She didn't turn to her boys as they approached the yard. Hearing them was enough, but who was with Ruthie and why was he walking, leading his horse? Three more strides and she knew—a bloody cloth around the mare's leg, a head bob at each step. It probably had gotten caught in some of that loose wire.

Haydock Carpenter made out the shapes—a man walking, a limping horse, that ugly Appaloosa the girl rode, the little thing perched up high. The black smelled something Haydock hadn't figured on—a lamed horse. As the black picked up a scent and spun toward the group, Haydock realized the bay was a mare. God damn.

Burn saw the wreck coming straight at him. An old man was pulling like a farmer on the open mouth of a young colt. Beauty was pulling the lead out of Burn's hand and spinning around on one foreleg, kicking hard at the colt, catching him in the jaw. The colt was staggering sideways as the Appaloosa, with the child yelling and yanking on him, pushed between the mare and the black and bit down hard on the black's neck, sending the colt backwards. The mare got in another kick and the colt went down, rolled over, then stood, trembling, shaking, riderless.

Ruthie slipped off the shaking roan. The old horse's ears were pinned back, his stub of a tail lifted, thrashing. With neck arched, the Appaloosa stomped a front hoof, clearly protecting the mare that stood close to him. Finding herself on her feet and safe, Ruthie ran for her mother.

Tad and Jonas roared into Burn, Tad swinging his rifle and connecting with Burn's raised arm. He grunted, grabbed the barrel, and pulled the kid to him, then slammed him in the ribs with his own rifle. The second wild boy poked Burn in the gut, and he countered with a slam at the barrel with the other boy's weapon. The boy stepped back, his face turning white as Burn easily picked the rifle out of his hands. He dropped both weapons and stood on them, digging the barrel ends into the dirt. He rubbed at his forearm and cursed the two fool kids.

It was a groan that made him turn. An old man was trying to sit up, grunting at each move. One leg was doubled back unnaturally under him and Burn saw, even as he walked over to the man, that the leg was broken. His head had been hit, blood dripping down. Burn knelt and spoke to the man, who stared up at him, and Burn understood.

Maggie Heber grabbed Ruthie and held her, watching the situation unfold. She grew furious that the boys had attacked the man, yet, in a way, glad that they had tried. What worried her was that they had been disarmed so quickly. She wanted to ask Ruthie who the man was that she had brought to the cabin, but her daughter, her beloved brave child, was crying. It was so unexpected that Maggie knelt down and just held Ruthie, holding the thin flesh, a heart beating too fast. Tears were wetting her dress, chilling her breast, and she held on tighter.

"You two, get over here," Burn snapped at the two boys.

Maggie wanted to stand at the stranger's words, but Ruthie pulled on her and said—"No, no."—

into her ear, so that Maggie hugged her closer and Ruthie cried harder.

Then from the stranger: "You pick him up . . . under his butt . . . and hold each other's arms at the elbow and wrist . . . make a chair, and don't you drop him. Watch the leg, it's broke."

"Where we taking him?" Jonas asked Burn.

"To the house. Do you think you're going to put him back on the horse? What do you mean, where?" Both boys looked at him blankly, as Burn pointed to the house. "You do know where you live, don't you?"

The boys managed to stagger up the two steps to the open front door and to maneuver Carpenter through the doorway without hitting the dangling leg on anything. The old man's head was resting on one boy's shoulder. Then the mother—at least she looked to be the mother of the two boys and the girl—got up, went inside, and started giving them directions, filled with warnings.

Burn let them disappear inside the house. He caught up the black colt, now nickering at the mare but wisely afraid to approach her. Blood dripped from his cut mouth, and, when the colt shook his head, droplets splattered his saddle and sweaty hide. The colt was cut between the hind legs, but the wounds were raw, too recent for instinct to have drained away. The colt whinnied at the mare, needing a warning or two from

Burn's hand on the bridle to remember his poor excuse for manners.

Burn bent to pick up the old man's hat, then steered the black colt toward the barn. The mare took one step, her head bobbing, and she stopped. The Appaloosa remained close to her, Beauty's brave protector. Burn called out to the girl, who was watching from the doorway, to help by holding on to the mare, patting her, and speaking to her until she was calm.

Good, Burn thought, *the child seems wise enough,* as she headed toward the mare. He didn't want the mare near the colt again.

Once they got out of the mare's reach, the black colt again snorted and pranced a few steps sideways toward Burn. Burn pulled quickly on the bridle reins and spoke to the colt, drawing his head around to one side, then pushing on the colt's neck until he lowered his head like a spanked child.

The little girl came up to Burn, face streaked with mud, eyes reddened. She explained she'd tied the mare to a fence rail so she could show him where he could put the colt. Her voice was thin, nothing like when she had yelled at him earlier.

"In here, we got a stall," she said, guiding him.

Burn unsaddled the black, hung up the gear, and couldn't help noticing the age of the Frazier rig, the fine quality of the woven blanket, and the beads of silver along the curb edge of the bit. Too bad that bit hadn't had more effect on the rank colt. He shoved an armful of hay into the one box stall.

"There a place I can put up the mare out a sight of this boy?" He immediately regretted his tone of voice, like the girl was a baby. He recognized the girl's look from those given by Elizabeth Hildahl, when her brothers teased her, or her sister Fanny when her mother wouldn't let her go to a dance.

"We got another corral out back . . . where we been keeping the cow."

"Show me," Burn said.

He followed her, and immediately started shaking his head. The corral was knee-deep in loose manure and urine pools. The stench was overwhelming. "Don't those boys know to keep the pens cleaned?" The child only looked at him so he tried to make it clear. "I can't put the mare in that mess, she'll infect the leg." He shook his head and turned back to the barn. When he got to the stall, he realized the girl had followed him.

"What're you gonna do?" she asked.

It would take thought and patience with this one, Burn realized, but he figured he had scared this child enough the past week or so. "My name's Burn English, child." He waited, looking at her.

"That don't answer my question."

Burn laughed. "You tell me your name, and then I'll answer."

"Oh."

Burn waited, knowing kids figured things out, mostly, if you let them have enough time.

"My name's Ruthie Heber, and this here's my home. You took my brothers' rifles away from them, and they're awful mad, but Ma won't let them hurt you."

They stared at each other, each holding onto something new.

Burn rubbed his face. "I'm going to put the colt in that pen. He'll be going home as soon as we can get word to his people. The mare'll go in here . . . least till we can get a clean pen for her. That answer what you wanted to know?"

He made the switch, giving the mare as much time as she needed to hobble inside the barn. He got her unsaddled and in the stall, and spread out more hay as bedding. She immediately laid down, and lipped at the hay with little interest. Burn found a pail, got some water, and went in the stall. He knelt down and offered Beauty water, which she played with, taking delicate sips and holding her mouth closed, swallowing and eventually pushing her muzzle deep into the bucket so that the water level was just below her eyes. Her actions meant she felt safe and that he could leave her alone now.

Then Ruthie started in with the questions.

"Why don't you leave the bucket with her? Ma wants me at the house now. You wanna come along?"

He held up the bucket, loosening the bail so it rang against the metal side. "You see this?" Burn asked. "You leave it in with a horse, on the floor, he gets a leg between this handle and the bucket and you got worse than that damned wire cut on the mare."

Her eyes were huge. "I better go."

She left Burn in the peace and quiet, the mare dozing at his feet, the colt outside squealing and doing nothing but getting himself filthy.

Burn got to the task of sorting out his own gear, making a nest for himself near the mare. He'd go to the house in a bit, when they had the old man settled, and find out what needed doing.

CHAPTER EIGHT

Maggie worked on Carpenter's head wound first after the boys had laid him out on her bed, not being too careful of his leg, but they were doing their best. She saw her sons' faces and tried to understand why they were so pale, their eyes fearful, their voices dimmed. She reckoned it was fear over the old man and what folks would say about the accident. Then she shook her head. Her reputation around here had been spoiled already by the bad-mouthing talk of the old man's wife. Nothing was going to change in a hurry.

Ruthie brought in the hot water she had put on the banked stove, having gotten the fire started and the kettle boiling, all without being asked. Maggie set a pan down next to the old man, who hadn't said much so far. He was in pain, that was obvious to anyone—his mouth was pulled tight, the muscles along his jaw twitched, but the biggest giveaway was the crooked leg, bent at a angle below the knee that just looked wrong.

She shook her head. Splints and wrappings were needed, but not quite yet. Her concern was the blood on his face, dripping onto his shirtfront and, if she didn't get him cleaned up, about to make a mess on her wedding ring quilt. Besides, he'd be more comfortable if the blood didn't dry on his skin. The simple task gave her time to prepare herself for what was to come next—his pain when the leg bone was straightened out. She couldn't count on the boys' help. It would fall to the man who had come in with Ruthie. Maggie wondered briefly who he was and where he'd gone? Ruthie would know.

As she washed the old skin, she was awed by the thin feel to it, by the blood vessels so close to the surface, by the papery scent that came from him stronger than the sweat from fear—the scent of blood. She'd never been this close to old age.

Her own folks had sent her off to be married, and she'd never seen them again. They were taken by a fever while she was struggling with her first husband on the eastern plains of Colorado. Fool place to try and farm, but he had insisted, since the government promised him free land if he homesteaded. So, by God, they would build a cabin and dig up the land for crops. Of course, there hadn't been any rain and the land had blown away and he had died of a fever after giving her the older of the boys—the ones who were gone now. She often thought of him, the best of her men, certainly better than Cal ever thought to be. And at least the boys wrote home to their ma once every year or so. Sometimes they even sent her a little money.

She felt the old man's hand reach around her fingers and she started, coming back to what she was doing, stopping her thinking about a past that wouldn't ever return. Sort of like the land that had blown away wouldn't ever return.

The bed on which they had laid the old man, Maggie's bed, was in a corner of the cabin, behind a layer of quilts hung from the beams to give her some privacy from Jonas and Tad. They slept close to the wood stove, for, in the winter, they were meant to keep it going even though they usually slept through the chore.

Ruthie had herself a loft in another corner, where she could read and hide and keep herself away from the roughhousing of her brothers. They knew never to go up into the loft. It was Ruthie's only refuge in their unconsciously brutal world.

The old man groaned, and Maggie laid her hand on his shoulder. He shrank away from her touch.

"Missus, you gotta help me," he muttered.

She patted the side of his face gently and felt only the slightest push against her hand. Briefly she had kind thoughts about the rancher. Then practicality got the best of her and she removed her hand, and left in search of rags to wipe up the blood. When she was back, she pressed very softly on the scrapes and the cut by his eyes. The old man shivered, but he did not complain.

Finally cleaned up and the simple wounds dressed, Carpenter opened his eyes. "Thank you, ma'am. I knew you were a good woman."

She smiled at the compliment even as her mind drifted. Pity his new wife didn't think the same way. Maggie looked away from him as she answered. "Mister Carpenter, now we got to set that leg. The man who come in with my daughter, she tells me he's kind." Maggie hesitated, fearing the pain she was about to cause. "I'll be needing his help."

Carpenter nodded, put his hand briefly on her wrist. "It's a bad 'un, missus. I knowed that since I tried to sit up out there. Damned colt . . . excuse me. I know . . . so you do what needs doing."

・・・

It was Ruthie who came for Burn, not saying anything but—"Ma. . . ." He nodded, then walked ahead of her to the log house. The woman opened the door. Burn recalled his manners—"Ma'am."— as he entered. The woman stepped aside for him and was behind him as they headed to the room's far corner and the brightly quilted bed. The old man was propped up with pillows and looking pretty spry, save for the busted leg.

The old man studied Burn, and then said: "Well, hell, you ain't much for causing all that ruckus."

Burn set him right. "It was you and the foolish colt you was riding. You cut him too late, rode him too soon."

The two men glared at each other.

Maggie thought she might have to get between them, like she did with her boys sometimes.

Finally the old-timer grinned, saying: "Hell, boy, you're right on that. Plumb foolish thing for me to do, but that colt . . . he's got fire and flash."

Burn disagreed. "Mister, you got a broke leg from the looks of it. Any colt'll be a fool and you know that. Didn't bother you much when you chose to ride him, but you're going to pay now." He remembered the bay colt he'd ridden almost to death one year and how that colt had kept his manners even near a female in heat. Youth wasn't any excuse.

Burn felt the woman beside him draw in a deep

114

breath before she spoke. "Who are you, mister, and what got you with Ruthie? My daughter won't say nothing 'bout you but she keeps talking about your pretty horse."

Burn didn't like the way Carpenter looked so interested, but the woman deserved an answer. After all, he was in her house, set up in her barn. "The name's Burn English. I don't know 'bout your daughter 'cepting she's been watching me for days without my knowing it, which makes me feel plumb foolish." He paused. "The mare got caught in wire, dammit, and I 'pologise, ma'am, but that wire's terrible stuff. Now I got me a lamed. . . ."

Carpenter spoke right over Burn's words. "So you're that son bred all those sorry bronc's down to New Mexico."

Burn took a deep breath, sensing the old man held a grudge against him. He took a gamble, but, from experience, he knew it was a safe bet. "Maybe you lost yourself a wager on one of my English horses, old man."

That got the rancher grinning. "Haydock Carpenter is the name, Burn English. You're smarter than you look to be. Yup . . . lost a thousand bucks and a good racing thoroughbred . . . bred in England, mind you, but he couldn't catch a dark colt out of your stallion. Learned my lesson that day. Ain't owned a racehorse since. Kept one stud for my use and bought me a couple of your good ranch horses, though, branded with your mark. And your training." The old man nodded his head. "Yeah, your training. Way you are, sonny, you'll recognize each one when my men coming riding in here, looking for me." Then Carpenter seemed to grow smaller and his face went pale and one hand drifted toward his chest before settling. The old man closed his eyes.

Burn pushed against the woman. "Best get to his leg, ma'am, before we wear him out."

She snapped at him: "You're the ones doing all the talking."

The woman had gathered sturdy poles and plenty of padding. Burn laid the sticks the length of the old man's leg, then broke off a few inches, rubbing the fresh cut against his pants to smooth the edges. The woman nodded at the old man's chest and between them they slid his body down the bed until he lay flat. The leg was twisted from the knee, no bone through the skin, but close, a bulge on the shin.

Burn slid a wide leather strap under the foot, pushed it up the calf to just below the bulge, then looked at the woman. She nodded her head once, her hands gripping the cloths. He raised the leg quickly, she slid the wrappings under the leather, and the old man bit down hard on his lip but didn't open his eyes.

Letting the leg come down, Burn snugged the poles, one on each side of the break, then raised the leg again while Maggie wrapped and pulled until the break eased into place with a grinding sound. Burn looked at the old man's face. It was white, sweaty. His eyes were shut, his breath hard, short. No complaints, though, no groan or cry.

Burn glanced at the woman. She, too, was white-faced, chewing at her lip, but, when she looked at Burn, her gaze was steady.

"It's in place now. You hold the foot and I'll tie off. Here. . . ." Maggie said, waiting.

Burn raised the leg, and Carpenter groaned out: "Son-of-a-bitch." Maggie tied a square knot with no further response from the injured man. There was blood on his mouth, caught in the cracked lip, at the corners, but still he made no sound.

Burn sat with Carpenter, who was sleeping now, head restless on the flattened pillow, his body rigid, knowing, even in sleep, that to move would bring agony. Behind him, Burn was conscious of the woman moving through her house and its chores with ease and a grace. He found that pleasing. Ruthie helped her mama, getting down pans and going out to what Burn figured was a root cellar. He grinned to himself as the child returned with an armful of orange carrots and a few potatoes.

The mother must have sensed his paying attention for she spun around. "You all suddenly dumping yourselves on us means we got to feed you and take from our winter stores. No one seems to have thought of what we're having to give up!"

He heard desperation above the raw anger and bitter tone. Then he realized it was an insult, and he thought to respond, but, thinking over her words, he reasoned she was right. He stood, careful not to wake the old man.

"You're right," Burn said. "Neither one of us thought to your provisions." He hesitated, scolding himself. "Ma'am." It came to him then. Her boys had come back with heavy rifles, but no food. If she was depending on her two sons, they'd all go hungry tonight.

A few strides and he was through the door, around the corner of the house and on to the barn. There he caught and cleaned up the old man's black colt and saddled the youngster with his own gear. He took the rifle from the old man's fancy rig and checked it for ammunition. There was enough, and the rifle felt better in his hands than had the battered old Winchester he'd been using for too many years. Then he went to climb up on the ungainly colt. The black threatened to buck out, but Burn was quick to feel the colt's mouth and put his legs to the shivering hide. Finally, after small arguments about direction and speed, the colt stepped forward into a stiff-jointed trot that would probably cause trouble with what had been healing in Burn's gut.

He settled the colt into a lope and headed north, over the rise at the back of the cabin where grasses grew knee-high and a few trees offered decent hiding. He slowed the colt after a half hour, noting that he now was willing to listen to Burn's commands. He eased the black to a halt by a stunted juniper and climbed down, tying the colt closely, while hoping he wasn't a talker.

It was pretty clear the boys hadn't gotten this far; their tracks had quit maybe twenty minutes back in a circle of flattened grasses where most likely they'd laid down and napped while thinking they were hunting game.

Burn walked through the grass to a distant setting of rocks and trees, holding himself quiet inside, easing his breath out in small puffs as he placed each step in the loose grass. The rifle rested easily in his hand, tucked under one arm, barrel down—not safe but when hunting he had to be ready.

Each step moved him closer to the rocks. Each time he stopped, a light wind touched his face as he listened to small *clucks* and *twitters*. Burn smiled; supper was waiting. Finally, so close it was almost sinful, the birds flew up, and he raised the barrel, following ahead of their panicky flight, firing quickly, and again, taking down one, two, even a third bird. He focused on where they landed, conscious of the rifle's new heat, the bending grass holding three small corpses.

Then the colt whinnied, twice, three times, as he pulled back on the reins, kicking out, tossing his head. *Not rifle-broke,* Burn decided, as he kept his eyes on where the birds lay waiting. He collected the birds.

Burn struggled getting on the colt, the youngster circling, still kicking out, eyes rolling at the sight and smell of the supper. *To hell with it,* Burn thought, and let the colt have his panicked gallop. At the top of the rise he hauled in the black, saw two young men running at him, one carrying a rusted shotgun. Her boys, a day late and a dollar short, on hearing distant rifle fire and a horse running at them.

Burn circled the anxious black as he held up the trio of birds, motioning for the boys to go back, which they did slowly, coming to a walk, then shaking their heads as they turned around. Burn watched them go to the cabin; the shotgun held in the one boy's grasp was unbroken, but still a potent weapon.

Maggie noted the birds with only the weakest of smiles, a slow headshake, no apologies, no thanks—just what Burn expected. "Outside" was all she said. He did his duty, gutting over a waste pit, then plucking the carcasses clean, removing the heads and feet, feeling the thin heat spread from their sticky blood into his hands. Warm, then cooling, plump breast meat, rounded thighs. Burn laughed, realizing he could be describing the woman inside that cabin, instead of a gutted meal.

Inside, he laid the birds in the iron skillet she had placed on the table. The tallow shone against the black metal. Herbs in a shallow wood bowl were bright green against the scoured grain. He hesitated as she kept her back to him, busy with something else. Burn sprinkled out the herbs, found a touch of salt near the stove, placed the fry pan on a hot empty place, and heard that satisfying *hiss* of heat against fat. He smiled, knowing she could hear yet would not give him the satisfaction of a response.

Sliced carrots, roasted potatoes, and three birds were divided among the six of them. Carpenter took a few sips of the broth water she'd boiled the carrots in before lightly toasting them in the greasy pan.

No one said a word. Heads bent, they all ate quickly, noisily, except for the woman, who leaned back at one point and released a huge sigh. The boys didn't react. The girl child's head jerked, and she leaned into her mother's side. The woman rested her hand on the child's head for a brief moment, then went back to her meal.

Burn hadn't tasted anything so good in a while. The herbs had worked magic, making each bite salty and sweet along with a tang from the bird tallow. The crisped skin of the birds was clean and sharp. Even the carrots, sweetened with molasses and lightly scorched, were a treat.

"Thank you, ma'am," Burn said. "That's a meal for a king you gave us."

Finally she looked at him, directly, her bitter eyes softened only a moment. "You hunt like that for us, mister, and you are welcome for a while. Only for a while, though. That clear?"

He nodded. "Yes, ma'am. It's a deal."

The next morning, when he came in, not too early, carrying a double brace of prairie chickens, the woman was seated at the stained table, both hands holding a tin cup. He could smell the coffee, and only had to glance at the stove where the pot stood, steaming, tempting, and she nodded, no words. An empty cup waited by the stove. He poured out the thick brew. She pushed an airtight of condensed milk across the table near a chair and Burn took the seat, accepting her gesture as an invitation.

He took a swallow, nodded in appreciation—thick, deep, bitter, and barely sweetened. Just the way he liked it. He took a long deep drink and wiped his mouth, put the cup down, careful not to make a sound.

"Mister, you're a rare one," Maggie said.

Burn raised his head just enough to glance briefly at her. She was smiling, and he grinned back. "I'll take that as a compliment, ma'am. Most folks call me something else and it ain't rare at all. More'n likely it's overdone, 'cause my mama was a good woman."

Her head jerked sideways, the slightest smile, opening her face, and for the first time her beauty was offered to him. But then that darkness returned. Her clear eyes clouded and the full mouth tightened to a bitter, too-knowing line. "What did you do to my daughter? Ruthie ain't stopped talking about you, and I don't trust a man 'round any female, especially my Ruthie, and you're one strange man. I don't want to be accusing too soon, so you can tell the truth or get the hell out of my house. Never mind your lamed mare and your hunting for breakfast."

His gut tightened and he would have walked out but for the child whose ma needed some comforting. "I rode north about a month ago. Not going no place in particular. I found that meadow, and the pond, and figured, since it weren't fenced, I could let the mare rest."

He shook his head, planted both hands flat on the table with a *crack,* forcing the woman to look at what he laid there for her to see. The backs of his hands told a story. Hard ridges of old flesh where wire had torn and healed.

"I hate wire," he said, hesitating, then: "Guess your child was watching me some . . . I never knew, though. Getting old . . . my senses ain't skilled or quick now. She was up there with that old Appy she rides, watching me. Doesn't make

me feel any too smart, but that's all there is."
He waited again, noting the woman's mouth
loosening, but her eyes remained hard. He
clenched his hands into fists, which whitened and
lifted the terrible scars. There was more he
needed to say, an apology of sorts. "Don't want
your child thinking most men look like me."

The woman snorted which he knew was a poor
attempt at not laughing. He pushed on, wanting
his say. "It ain't my height or size . . . it's the
scarring. My hide's in a bad way, and most folks,
well, they don't keep living cut up this way. You
need to tell her I ain't the usual sort of man." That
hadn't come out the way he meant it to, sounding
more like bragging, and his face got warm. He
wanted to start all over again, try to get her to
understand what was bothering him.

Instead, her hand came out and one finger
traced the ugliest of the scars on his hand.

Burn flinched, almost pulled back, but the
touch didn't hurt this time. Even if he touched
that scar, he felt a twist in his gut that made him
dizzy. Her touch was gentle. It was the same way
he handled a skittish horse.

She spoke, surprising him. "Wire?"

He pulled back his hand, hesitated. "Yes."

"So what scared my Ruthie is true. The rest of
you . . . ?"

Burn dropped his head, found his mouth dry. He
barely nodded.

"Oh." Then a blank space where no thoughts or words would fit. "I'll tell her when she gets talking 'bout you and that mare again. I promise." Her voice had gone soft, and to Burn it felt like forgiveness. "Damn." Her final word, his choice, too, but he couldn't speak it, not deliberately in front of her.

The woman stood, pushed away from the table. "Let's get them birds gutted and plucked. You did a fine job last night." She returned the stiffening bodies to him, saying—"Here."—and Burn was glad for the excuse to get away from her and the cabin walls.

One of the boys approached him as he yanked viciously at the stubborn feathers. His first reaction was to throw the carcass at the kid's head. Attacking him with a rifle—hell, this whole family was crazy, and dangerous.

The kid grunted. Burn kept plucking.

"Mister." As if one word would cause Burn to leave off his chore to listen.

"Mister!"

"The name is English, sonny." He thought a moment. "Then again your sister and probably your ma already told you that. You don't know much about behaving with your elders, now do you, boy." He made it a statement, not a question, but the skinny kid was rough and readied to fight, having learned his early manners from his ma, and the rest from his brother. The rudeness was a choice.

"You been taught better, boy," Burn stated. "Mind what your ma tells you or you'll get a lot more than a fight."

The boy stepped in, too close, and Burn reached out, slapped the beardless face, and sent the boy spinning. He dropped one of the birds. "No threats to me, boy. You got no rifle and you can see this knife I'm holding. Don't go for a fight when the opponent's already better armed."

Burn picked up the dirtied carcass, wiped off most of the dirt specks, and finished pulling out the last of the feathers. He paid no attention to the kid who stayed flat on the earth for a few moments, watching Burn closely. Then he stood, backed himself up a few steps, coughed, and wiped his mouth.

"Mister English, my ma says can you bring her the birds. She's got the pan hot."

Burn pulled out the last feather, then stared straight at the boy. He wasn't bad-looking, rough in the face right now, and the lank hair in his eyes didn't improve what looks he did have, but the size was there in the broad hands, shoulders to match, a length of leg that Burn purely admired. He'd been a runt so long, from that fever that had taken his whole family, that he still got a twinge when he saw promise in a kid like this. And anger when the kid acted a fool.

"Here." He handed off the birds with forced politeness, feeling their stickiness on his fingers and arms. Gutting was an unpleasant chore he hated but did without thought or feeling. It was about survival, either his or the birds', and that made it not much of a choice.

"Thanks, Mister . . . ah . . . English."

Burn had to grin as the kid loped off toward the house, birds hanging from his big hands, bouncing against his thigh and ribs. *Baby boy filled with wanting to be a man,* thought Burn.

He went to the well pump, ducking his head under the faucet as he worked the handle. Couldn't get clean enough this way, but it was better than walking back to the pond. He gasped, drew in the icy water, and spat it out, trying to get the bird taste washed from him.

The everyday act of killing never had gotten easy for him, and that last remembered shot, shattering the stallion's head, driving life and years from the horse's lungs and heart, had almost made him willing to eat grasses and leaves rather than kill one more time. But life didn't work that way. Nothing in life was directed toward saving another. It was about eating or getting bit in two for some bear's dinner. Burn shook his head, felt wet hair slap him, and tried to laugh to mock the foolishness of his turning soft in old age. Instead, he stood up, shuddered, and felt his heart pounding too hard inside his chest. *Too old* was a chant he heard in his sleep. *Too late* a challenge he couldn't face.

She had the birds sliced and frying when he knocked. She didn't turn, merely flipped over a side of white meat and spoke her piece. "You come in, Mister English. Could you see if Carpenter will eat a few bites?" Then there was a hesitation, a softening of her voice. "Thank you again for the birds." She handed him a plate.

If she could know the turmoil going on inside him over the act of providing for her, she'd laugh, call him a fool, send him on his way. He would best keep his mouth shut.

Carpenter was awake, so Burn sat in the nursing chair, speaking gently. "Mister Carpenter, she cooked this up just for you."

There was no movement except for a flutter of the heart visible in his chest, a slow unregulated pounding that echoed what Burn felt. He let the moment drift by, holding the plate with three small bits of soft chicken, warm and moist, their scent rising to tempt even Burn.

Then: "Fine." A whisper that made Burn's head jerk. This was a task he'd never undertaken. He'd been hand-fed himself before, could still see Katherine's hand holding a spoon, trying desperately to tempt him. The image faded when Burn saw the old man looking at the spoon, then at Burn's marked hand.

The words were barely audible as Carpenter's voice croaked: "Ain't never had chicken fed to me for breakfast 'fore this. Prefer coffee and eggs . . . fresh tortillas."

Burn laughed, then steadied himself and offered a chicken bite on the front edge of a broad spoon. The old man opened his mouth, a maw empty of half its teeth. Gingerly, trying to avoid the white spines of the front jaw, Burn slipped in the piece. He watched the jaw close and heard the cautious chewing. Then it stopped, then more chewing, then nothing. Finally a deep sigh. Carpenter closed his eyes. Too much work to eat. Burn knew because he'd felt those small pains take hold. It was hard on a man to admit he couldn't do for himself.

"That's right, Mister Carpenter. Gotta eat when you can. Food ain't always right in front of us. Living hard taught us both that same lesson, if nothing more." He thought there was a nod, a slight dip of the bony skull, a glint to the half-closed eyes as the mouth opened. Bits of chewed flesh stuck to the lower lip.

"More?"

Again almost a nod. The spoon slipped under the chicken bite, slid into the maw easily, and Burn tipped the utensil, felt the tongue gather in that small morsel, and both men sighed. It was an unnatural act for them, a dependency and delicacy neither liked to admit in themselves.

One more bite and the jaw hung loosely. The eyes were closed, and that pounding, lifting heart seemed eased, soothed by nourishment into a quiet sleep.

Burn's back ached when he stood and left the bedside. The woman turned to him, smiling now, a true and breathtaking smile. He handed her the small plate, the spoon, and still she smiled.

"Mister English, that was one of the kindest things I've seen a man do. The two of you . . . like you'd known each other for years."

Burn couldn't quite get his breath. He shrugged, looked out the door. "He's gotta eat, ma'am. Pride makes it tough on him . . . being laid up and all." She cocked her head. He shrugged again. "I know . . . that's all."

He scrambled from her smile, her face, the sweetness in her eyes. He needed to check on the mare, wash out that wound, and re-bandage it, rinse out the old shirt rags, see if the wound's heat was still bad. Maybe, somehow, he could soak the leg in cold water—a bucket from the well pump, a hand rag, anything to keep him busy for an hour or so.

CHAPTER NINE

The face came in and out of view. A rough face. A scruffy beard. A damned fool who needed to shave, and get that hair shortened so a good man could trust him. Looks like some kind of a horse thief . . . that's what it was. The black colt . . . a mare . . . and then he couldn't remember any more. But it was about horses. Always about horses. Or women. Damn the both of them for being in a man's life.

The face wasn't familiar, though. He couldn't register the who and why. His leg hurt. By God, it was on fire most of the time. So he slept. Delirious more than likely, but it was an escape he could manage. Still couldn't place the face, and it bothered him some.

He ate the chicken. It tasted like sawdust and some sweet herb—wild fowl, hard, stringy, but salted well. The unfamiliar man fed him, his hand shaking almost as much as Haydock's chest pounded. But he got the food in. Wasn't really chicken even though Haydock swore that's what the man had called it. But it was flavored enough to keep him interested.

The woman was damned pretty. Younger than

his wife and had a better figure. Even in a damned plain dress and an apron, her figure filled a man's eye, got him to thinking of better things.

Haydock wished the woman would do the feeding, but he knew why she didn't. The man had the patience. He'd sit his skinny rump in that wood chair and let his head droop, waiting, hands still on the plate, spoon never moving until he was ready. Nervy son-of-a-bitch, but he was careful with that spoon, could take out one of the few teeth left in his mouth if he didn't pay attention. Haydock watched the hand come closer to him, so close that he could no longer see it but could feel it touch his lips. The hands were scarred badly, the hands of a man who had lived his life doing hard work.

Scars. Haydock knew what it was to be useless, hurt, down, and in a bad way. And now unable to hold a damned spoon to his own mouth. Horses, ropes, wire, fast horses, and lost bets. Damn.

Later, maybe midday, he grunted and sort of raised his own skinny behind. The man understood, and blushed like a parlor whore as he spoke in murmurs to the woman. She handed him a large shallow bowl. Her voice was loud. It was all she had. It would be the old man's till he left, then they'd scald it clean from his waste. Haydock knew she meant well, but it was reminding him again he was dying. Wouldn't be long.

The skinny horseman, he tried to hush the woman and that was a mistake. She rested both hands on her hips and got wagging at him and he backed up, holding the bowl, bumping into a chair, and came around to stare at Haydock.

No words were said, but there was insult and fury in the dark face, and Haydock admired the man's gumption. Then it was time to remind him of the why for the fussing. His body needed relief, he wanted to tell the skinny man now hunched over him. Embarrassment stunk from the man's skin, his hot breath on Haydock's belly, but they managed the need and it wasn't too bad. Some kind of curtain was pulled around the bed to shield the rest of the family from his act, especially the little girl. Haydock had no trouble with that. It was the man's turned face, his ice-cold hands on Haydock's wilted flesh that brought out a laugh, and he felt the man flinch. He mumbled—"Sorry."—and hoped it was enough.

"I'm the one sorry, Mister Carpenter," the man said. "I ain't usually this stupid or clumsy."

Damned strange time for an apology, helping a dead man piss.

It was in him already, waiting. Deep in a once-strong heart, a hole, widening with each breath. His ribs barely rose and fell. His heart labored to keep living. Haydock held his eyes open, wanting to look into this stranger's face and know who would sit by him when it came.

"Your name?"

"I told. . . ." The voice cut itself off, acknowledging the beginning of complaint.

Haydock grinned. "I can guess, boy. You tole me enough times, but then my head ain't been too clear." He took the risk, curious. "My heart, neither." That hit. The man ducked his head. He knew, and that knowing allowed Haydock to relax. Again: "Your name?"

"Burn English, Mister Carpenter."

He heard the name, remembered having recognized it. "Your bay colt beat my racer," Carpenter said.

Both men grinned. They shared a past even though they stood as strangers. Carpenter got it out—"Damn' good horses."—before drifting off to sleep.

Burn was careful marching out of the cabin—the cracked china bowl filled with red-stained urine—and on to the outhouse where he kicked open the door and caught one of the boys doing to himself what he'd probably just learned felt good. Burn bellowed for the kid to get the hell out of his way. The whole damned place was mad he realized as the kid bolted, pants down to his knees, drawers flapping, wide open.

His errand done, Burn spent a good ten minutes cleaning his hands, then his face, under the cold pump water. He could breathe again, lick his lips, and taste the good water, take in air and smell the grasses, even the moist dirt around the pump. He was cleansed.

He went to check on the mare, noticing on the way the long shadows and feeling the winter-chilled air blowing close to the ground, stopping the grass, slowing the trees, shutting down the land before the first snow.

Studying the wire wound, he saw the edges had thickened. The open flesh was bright pink. *Good,* he thought, *no infection, not impossible to keep clean.* He chilled the leg again, applying cold water with a fistful of clean rags the woman had given him. The mare winced, tried to pull away. She relaxed when she began to feel the effects of the cold. She let her head rest on top of Burn's shoulder and even took hold of his shirt, fabric between her teeth, quiet, eyes half closed. A peace that surprised Burn. He didn't remember wire being this way.

Done, he wrapped the leg, taking extra care as he placed the material on the open flesh. Still the mare was quiet, her head bobbing against his arm, muzzle rubbing on his shoulder. A week at the most and he could leave, leading the mare, maybe, but he could get out of this hell.

Haydock hadn't come home last night, and at midday there was still no sign of the black colt calling down to the pens. Rose Carpenter was disgusted, annoyed, and, if she admitted it to herself, worried some about what fool thing Haydock might have done this time.

They had been married two years now, and all his promises hadn't been kept yet, so he damned well better not be dead, or something else. Better not be with that woman, Maggie Heber, or whatever her last man's name had been. Haydock had said he was riding out to look at the grass damage. Him and his damned grass, worrying on it, instead of staying home and keeping his wife happy.

His old eyes and rough hands found what they wanted in her flesh, and she was willing to give up to him anything he wanted. It wasn't often, or for long, but her willingness made him feel young he said. He had told her she could fancy up the house and buy herself clothes that made her look like a lady and even get a carriage painted in new colors with a team of matched bays—whatever she wanted. It was a fair bargain for them both. Better than what she'd thought would come to her.

Not bad for a woman of her age and disgrace. A man to pay the bills and give her comforts, maybe even leave her a few dollars when he died. The old coot, where was he? He was all she had now, a fattening woman no one else wanted. He was everything to her.

Rose grabbed a shawl and went down to the

corrals, sweeping up the useless long full skirt to get where she was going more quickly. It might look pretty, but, by God, all that material got in her way, and, if she fell on her face, she would get nothing but jeers and catcalls. The Rafter JX hands didn't like her. She could tell by their cold gazes and mutterings as she walked by. But, damn them, she'd earned all this; it hadn't been easy letting men pay for her favors.

Rogelio was standing at the empty corral. He nodded to her, saying—"*Buenas días, señora.*"— in that polite deep voice of his. She smiled before remembering why she was standing in horse shit and dried leaves, staring at an empty space.

"He didn't come home." Her voice was flat, no lightness. Plain fact. The Mexican nodded once, then wiped his mouth with his hand, and for that Rose cursed him and all males who thought a woman only good for one thing. Then Rogelio told her what she had come down to the pens to hear.

"I sent Arcy out to follow the tracks, *señora*. He is our best at such things."

He was worried enough about her husband that his voice had a tremble. Rose turned to look at him. His face in profile had an arched nose and heavily lidded eyes, a wide mouth pulled down at the corners. A strong face, with a dignity surprising to Rose. Men like Rogelio had not come into the places she had worked. They were not welcome because of their dark skin, mixed Indian and Mexican blood.

"The *señor*, he is proud, and that black colt helps him remember he is still a man."

She knew Rogelio knew Haydock pretty darned well, guessed they had worked together maybe fifty years. His comment fit with her speculations.

Rose drew in a quick breath, let it out in short puffs. She wanted to tell the man that it was her job to make Haydock feel like the man he used to be, in those intimate moments—that's what she was paid for. To her the horse and all that male bragging only made Haydock seem foolish. Silly that he would need to show off his skills in subduing the colt.

"Do you know where he went?" she asked, all the while brooding over Maggie Heber.

The Mexican shook his head. "I think, *señora*, that he would ride south to where a man has been staying in Salt Valley, the place you like so much. The *señor*, he does not want anything you like to be spoiled by others."

He kept talking, but the words dissolved as she thought of that one fact: Haydock actually listened to her. She wanted a house in that valley. She had never seen such a place before. That Haydock remembered and might want to ride there and check it out. *Ah,* she thought, *he's taking care of me.*

138

"Well why don't you send a rider to the valley, if that's where you think he went?"

Rogelio shook his head. "*Señora*, if he did not go to the valley and we ride there, we have lost time. It is a waste. Arcy will find him by following his tracks. Please have patience."

Rose glared at the man, who had nerve to smile at her—no civility, not the behavior of a ranch hand to the boss' wife—a fine open smile proclaiming his range superiority. She raised her hand, studying him closely. She saw no fear, no worry, and carefully brushed a strand of hair off her forehead. This man was certain of the choice he had made and would not bow to her demands.

"I will tell the boss what you have decided, *Señor* Rogelio, and how his life depended on the rightness of that choice." She tried to be formal, direct, perhaps threatening, and still he smiled as he reminded her: "Arcy will find him."

Haydock was sleeping now, so Maggie returned to her chair near the fire. Her second husband had made the chair and it suited her to rock in it, thinking of him, and life in general.

Life was a pickle right now—one man housebound on her bed, her two boys angry and taking it out on whatever they touched. This morning Tad had broken two railings on the corral fence and she'd sent him out to cut and bring in replacements, without his noon meal. The boy had responded with a sullen and miserable attitude so she had had to be firm. She had stepped close to him, patted his cheek with one hand, and told him he best do the chore to make up for his foolishness, or he was gone off the property. Love didn't matter, he had to pull his weight, and it was no good asking Jonas to do the job, he'd not broken the rails.

Jonas was down at the corrals, trying to clean the pens the way Burn English had told him they should be cleaned. She hadn't been down there in a long time, having depended on the boys to tell her they'd done the job right. She was downright disgusted that her boys had let the pens get so filthy, but there it was. Now Jonas was pitching manure over the fence into a good size pile, complaining all the while.

Burn English. Skinny and not much to him. Hard to figure him out. No posturing or bragging to make himself important. He had a way of knowing that even Maggie recognized, a way of looking at a problem and setting about a solution, like helping her set old man Carpenter's broken leg. She hadn't known to raise the leg and slide in those splints. She would have laid sticks alongside and tried to tie off even if she'd hurt him, not knowing what else could be done except hope that he passed out and suffered the doctoring unconscious.

A lot of gray was in Burn's wild black hair. And

his pale green eyes spooked her when he swung around and was so close she could look straight into them. His skin was dark from the sun, she figured, for she'd seen his pale chest and the marked line at his neck. The darkness made those pale eyes glow. His white skin looked smooth going down into his tattered shirt. Except, of course, for the scars, which she'd glimpsed on his forearm and those others that Ruthie had told her about with eyes wide and fearful, already knowing that such marks meant suffering. She still needed to keep her promise to him, and tell Ruthie that not all men were so scarred. She liked that about him, his wanting to make sure her child wasn't scared.

When she stood next to him, Maggie realized she had to look down at him—shorter than her by a good two inches—yet he didn't try to make up for that lack by any nonsense most men would, posing and wearing a tall-crowned hat, those thicker boot heels. Nothing like that in him at all.

He was pure, unlike the men who usually came sniffing around, making comments and asking if she had a man and did she want one for a while in her bed. She'd never met a man who hadn't tried something with her. And she didn't want to understand the why, not now, not at her used-up age.

Looking in the tin mirror, the boys used for occasional shaving, she saw lines and wrinkles and gray strands in her own dark hair, a neck beginning to wrinkle. She knew too well the flesh under her plain dresses was marked from bearing each child. But the men still came around, like Mr. Carpenter riding up to show off, and then breaking his leg, maybe even bringing about his own death. Maggie wasn't going to take on that burden. Still, she was saddened by his pain, hearing him curse in the night, bathing him as best she could, even with him watching her, sometimes touching her hand when she washed his face.

Mr. Carpenter, he was a full-length man. His fingers were long and blunt, his nails ragged. Creases and wrinkles told of a hard life. Work hard, make do. But he had gotten lucky and rich, hawking cattle to the railroads, the cities, and now he had bedded a younger woman, fleshy and foul-mouthed. And still he came around Maggie.

His touch was gentle, not tense with desire, an old man's hand on hers, rough skin thanking her—a thumb on her wrist, fingers against her forearm, the tips missing on two of them. And when she smiled, his mouth lifted in the smallest of gestures. Once, without thinking, Maggie had leaned over and kissed the stubbled cheek, and the old man had grinned. She had felt the effort under her mouth and it gave her a sense of wonder. His smell had stayed on her lips—heat, sour, and something terribly wrong. She knew it wasn't just the break, that it was something else.

This morning she had sent Ruthie on the old roan to the Rafter JX to tell someone there what had happened, hoping it wouldn't end up being the harridan wife. Perhaps she could tell Rogelio Vigil, or one of the other hands, that their boss was banged up and over at the Heber place. She would let them figure out how and when to move him, or send for a doctor in Mancos, or even up in Pueblo or Cañon City. Maybe the old man's life could be saved.

She feared her place was going to get crowded soon, with too many voices and opinions, and Maggie wanted only to step back and let the others fight it out. It was the old man's choice, his life, but Maggie guessed the wife would have her own ideas.

It would be simple enough to cart him home in a wagon bed and mourn him when the ugly leg break erupted and took his life. The wife could blame Maggie, the ranch hand who would drive the wagon, the team of horses. She would blame everyone except herself.

The rocker slowed and Maggie leaned forward, looking out the window where she caught sight of Burn English walking from the barn. He stopped at the pump, put his head under the icy flow, and came up blowing out, hands pulling through his hair trying to comb through the tangles. She might offer a haircut; it would be an

143

easy enough chore for her to do. Those birds he'd been shooting, well, they had tasted right good with the seared carrots and potatoes, and she wanted to find a proper way to thank him.

CHAPTER TEN

The rider was young, not a whole lot older than Ruthie, but she didn't like him telling her what she should do. If she was riding to the Carpenter place, no man had the right to stop her. She challenged him with that fact and he tried to explain, but Ruthie had her orders and pulled Roany around the pretty-looking spotted sorrel the man rode and kicked her bronco into a staggering trot.

He called out after her, but Ruthie chose not to listen. The child could have told him about Carpenter—what had happened, where he was—except for her stubbornness. Her ma's words stayed with her: *You get to that ranch house and don't let no one stop you. You tell that woman where her man is.* Exactly what Ruthie would do.

She was a child, pretty enough, but a baby really, too young for Arcy's interest, but she could ride and had a temper. He admired her ability with a horse, but she didn't appear to be a good listener.

When he was excited or confused, English did not always make sense to Arcy. He tried to tell her that he was back-tracking *Señor* Carpenter and following the black colt's trail. But she just rode off in silence.

Arcy stood in the stirrups, letting loose on the rein, and the paint stepped into an easy lope, then a slow gallop, ears pricked, moving quickly without fear of the holes hidden by high grasses, ignoring the wandering trail of cattle hoofs and slow broodmares.

Arcy reined in at the low ridge, looking down on the cabin. As he slowly approached the house, he could make out a series of tracks that told him a bad story. A confrontation between a number of horses, including the small girl's roan—one of the horses had gone down—footprints of a number of people, including some small ones, more than likely those of the girl. Some marks indicated that someone had been carried toward the house, and Arcy's gut told him it had been the old man.

He hesitated, letting the sorrel paint spin a tight circle. A loud shout made him look to the right where he saw a boy running at him, a rifle held at his waist, yelling words Arcy could not make out. Then, stumbling, the boy went down and rolled over, and the rifle fired once. Arcy's paint half reared against the tight rein, and Arcy had the humiliation of grabbing for the saddle horn. As he let the paint settle, he studied what was before him. The fallen boy now stood, rifle pointed to the ground, and even at this distance his face showed to be pale, which made Arcy grin. This was another young one who thought he could take on anything, especially with that rifle.

A second boy, he looked to be the older of the two because of his stride, came to the side of the other. Next a woman was at the cabin door, hand above her eyes to shade them against the sun. Her voice was pitched high, but he could not make out the words. From the way the boys abruptly turned, Arcy decided they were being scolded. The boy who had fallen pointed toward Arcy.

Then the child charged, dragging the rifle as he bolted toward the Rafter JX hand. The woman screamed something, and the boy slowed. It was then that Arcy decided he, too, was being childish and let the paint pick his way to the cabin. The woman stepped out to meet him.

Arcy slid gracefully off the paint and took one step toward the woman, half bowing as he removed his hat. This was why the old man's tracks led to the cabin with its filthy pens, the cow and its slobbering calf.

Even though the *señora*, for the girl was her child, as were the two hulking boys who ran up beside her, was twice Arcy's age, her eyes were wide and knowing, and her face quite beautiful.

Her body . . . such a body cried out for man to stroke it. In the boys, who looked so much like her, the facial features showed a lack of depth and appeared all too feminine. The mouths were too wide, the lips too red, too full—on her they were alluring, on the male children they appeared as a flaw.

Arcy realized she was speaking to him over the pounding of his heart and he nodded as if understanding. Slowly the words began to make sense.

"You scared us," the woman said. "My boys were only trying to protect me. Don't be hard on them." Then she smiled and he knew he would do whatever she asked of him. "Don't blame the boys, *señor*. Their hearts are good if their aim is god-awful."

He laughed, unsure if she really meant the words for she seemed to be apologizing for the fact that they had not shot him. Once again he politely bowed and heard one of the boys laugh, but Arcy did not care. The woman's smile was enough reward. But he must attend to the business that had sent him on this miserable errand.

"*Señora*." He made the polite address, even though he knew she had had several men living with her. "I have come seeking *Señor* Carpenter. He is here?"

Her face sobered but still she was lovely,

147

although her age became more obvious and he revised his guess to be more than twice his age. He was eighteen, almost nineteen, and she had to be over forty.

Her sigh told him what he wanted to know before she began to speak. "Yes. That black colt of his stampeded and fell. Mister Carpenter has broken his leg. He's inside, if you would like to visit him."

Then a man appeared. A horseman, this one. It was easy to tell by his walk and the breadth of his hands, the worn boots. Older, too, like the woman, but his eyes held a different fire. As he approached, the sorrel paint turned snorty, and Arcy had to tug on the bridle to quiet the gelding.

The man walked to Arcy without a word and put his hand on the paint's neck. The horse bowed his head to an open hand, snuffling and then licking the fingers, the exposed palm. Arcy went to jerk on the reins but felt the man's hand hold against his movement. They stared at each other. Arcy's attention was drawn away from the woman to what he assumed would be a more difficult challenge.

The man's voice was pitched low when he spoke, and the sorrel paint nickered. "He's done nothing wrong, son. You can let up on his mouth . . . now."

It was a command, given softly but without mistake. Those eyes held danger, and Arcy felt his face turn red as his hand opened quickly and the reins slid through, falling to the ground. The paint took a small step and leaned his head on the man's outstretched arm.

"I raised this one," the man said. "His ma was a prettily marked mustang. He don't need yanking on his mouth 'less you already ruined him with your riding, *señor*."

It was an insult but the truth. Arcy had been told by Rogelio and the *señor* himself that his hands were too strong, too harsh with the horses. Bit and reins were used only for asking, and always with kindness, never as punishment. He looked down and away, not wanting to see the man's hand, the strong wrist, the terrible marks that Arcy recognized. His father had had similar scars, and Arcy remembered his painful journey through life and a long lingering death.

He picked up the reins and offered them to the man, careful not to look into those eyes. But the gift was rejected, left hanging, so Arcy dropped the leather, and the sorrel snorted, shied back a step. But the man's soft voice came as a command—"Whoa."—and the sorrel planted his feet, raising a cloud of dust. Arcy sneezed, then apologized. It was becoming clear he had much to learn.

The women stepped forward, as if the man was not there, saying: "You come in and talk to your boss, iffen he's not sleeping. Won't have you wake him . . . sleep's the best thing for him right now. Sleep and some quiet." Here she glared at her two sons, who were keeping their distance, their faces uniformly displaying anger and fear. "Shooting at strangers ain't quiet," she reminded them.

The cabin was clean, that was his first observation as he followed the woman inside. Her body moved precisely, telling any full-blooded man that she knew what he was seeing and appreciating. The table was scoured almost white, ridges of hard grain rising above softer surfaces. Arcy let his hand rest on the surface, feeling each bump, knowing how this family lived. He inhaled deeply, tasted something salty-sweet in the air, and he had to swallow.

Then she said to him: "Over here."

Arcy drew in a new smell, his mouth puckering, and he breathed heavily. She pulled back a thin curtain.

Carpenter did not stir.

Gone a day, and he looked old, ancient to Arcy's young eyes. Mouth drawn down, white stubble sagging in his wrinkles. His eyelids were bluish and so thin Arcy felt he could see the eyes beneath them. His eyes trailed to a broken leg, bound in filthy rags against two sticks. He'd done such wrapping with an *amigo* who never walked or rode again. *Would have been better if he had died* was the thought that flashed through his mind, which he knew was wrong to think.

He spoke quietly, not knowing if his boss would hear or not. "¿*Señor*?" Once, then a second time as his hand touched the stained quilt. A third time and Carpenter's eyelids slid back, revealing the depths of his soul it seemed to Arcy.

"Boy." Low, wavering much like a bird's song. A tremble rarely heard in such a strong *hombre*.

Arcy felt his throat close, his eyes sting. He struggled to find the words. "*Señor*, Rogelio, he asked me to come find you . . . the colt. These people are caring well for you." He gestured stupidly at the wrapped leg, and the old man grunted. "Your wife, the *señora*, worries . . . but now I can tell her you are resting." Not all of his words were true but rather the kinds of things one must say to keep the old man from knowing the truth. Death was already in this house, the ghost who came for the spirit.

Carpenter made the effort to roll his head and look straight at Arcy, and it was a wonder of will and strength. The old man could feel it in his chest, but mostly in his heart—a flutter that he had occasionally felt before but which was now constant and, in his tired mind, a welcoming sign.

Arcy realized the *señora* soon would have what she wanted, and the ranch hands, too, would get their portion of cash as the old man had promised. This kindness would buy the *señor* some peace.

The man who knew horses stood behind Arcy,

his eyes glittering as he studied Carpenter. He cocked his head at the old man.

The old man understood that look, nodded as if saying, yeah, he wanted the visitor gone. Let him sleep, he had nothing more to prove.

Burn let his hand rest lightly on Arcy's shoulder, and the youngster turned to him. The young man's dark eyes were wide open, his face pale. Even with a gentle touch Burn could feel him shiver. He tugged and the boy followed Burn away from his sleeping boss.

"He is going to die?" It was a question, but Arcy already knew the answer.

Burn nodded, and Arcy's torso bunched as he turned his head. *"Ahhh."*

Burn looked at the cabin floor, kicked at a clump of manure, most likely dragged in on his own boots. He, too, was restless, wanting to bolt from the cabin. It wasn't his place. He didn't know the people—the old man, the scared *vaquero*, the ill-tempered sons, and the girl child. But he knew the truth. He stayed because the woman had looked at him with her clear eyes and half smiled and sighed when he had taken over dealing with Carpenter's rider. He nodded at her, seated in her chair. Now her head tilted and Burn lost his breath. No one looked at him like that, not since he first had met Katherine Donald before she married Davey Hildahl.

The woman was too pretty, too sure of herself

not to know the effect of her smile, so he scolded himself, tried to hold back his interest. She had three children, maybe more, so there were husbands—or just men. He was being unkind in his thoughts about her in an effort to remind himself of what he was. Old, set in his ways, on the losing end of his life, not at the beginning when a smile from a woman made one an instant fool. Katherine had done that to him, staggered his heart with a look, and he would not let it happen again.

He wrapped his arm around the young *vaquero*'s shoulders and walked him outside into the fresh air and the brightness that belied what hovered inside the cabin walls. "Boy, you ride back and try to explain to his wife. It was an accident, pure and simple. That black colt did for the old man . . . trying to mount an unwilling mare. That colt's fresh cut, an' the desire is still there." Burn saw understanding come over the boy's face and decided to give him some direction. "He needs manners taught to him, boy. Not through a harsh bit and spurs, but through lots of work . . . long rides checking fence, and then resting, tied and hobbled. Keep him sweaty and tired, and he'll make a decent mount." The boy nodded, so Burn continued. "Circle him when he gets stiff in the jaw. Ain't no good putting in a hard bit, he'll brace on you and the son can bolt."

A lot of words. Why was it that people always

needed something from him—help or advice he wasn't fit to give. As for children. Well, a kindness to a child had always been hard for him. Even Katherine's children had known he wasn't one for niceties, but they had come to him with horse questions and school problems, which he had found an odd pleasure when they weren't pestering him to death. He was hip-deep in the same mess again and only gone a few weeks. It was almost funny. Now this kid was confused, but it was only about horses.

Burn sort of pushed Arcy toward the paint. "Think on it, son. Horses ain't the enemy. We are."

The words rode with Arcy as he headed the sorrel paint back toward the Rafter JX. He had not understood all of the man's instructions, for that was what it had been, a lesson. He had heard it before from others, and now it had come from the man who had created this wonderful horse Arcy was allowed to ride. The horse he had tried to buy from *Señor* Carpenter.

This time, perhaps, he would listen, and try to feel, rather than just yanking and grabbing. But when he felt a weight in the reins and the horse bowed his neck and chewed at the bit, Arcy's fists got hard and that delicate feel went away until he let the strength in his elbow release and the paint chewed again.

It was most peculiar. He wasn't sure of what use this gesture had been, until he turned to look at the rump end of a disappearing pronghorn, and, at the same time, the paint turned underneath Arcy, and seemed to be waiting for him. He could feel the paint's hindquarters bunch with power, and briefly he thought of chasing the pronghorn. At that second the paint leaped forward. So Arcy let the horse run for a half mile, and he threw back his head, letting the hat slip off and hang from its leather strand. He laughed as the paint dodged trees and cactus and seemed to be catching up with the little pronghorn buck. Next he thought about slowing down and the paint eased into a lope. The touch on the reins weighed almost nothing and yet the paint came to a walk and then stretched out his neck, and Arcy let him take the reins until his walk was long and even.

When the ranch house was in sight, Arcy felt both pleasure because of the lesson he had just learned about the paint and disappointment because of the information he must give to the *señora*.

CHAPTER ELEVEN

For the first time Ruthie really understood the ugliness of the roan Appaloosa. His ears were too long—his face looked silly because of the white surrounding both blue eyes—his mane stood straight up, and his tail was thin and straggly so that, once when she had tried to braid it, the hairs wouldn't hold a ribbon. Even his color was wrong—sort of three or four colors all mixed together, making him look like a mistake.

She patted his neck nervously as he swung his big head around, almost knocking over Mrs. Carpenter, who had come out to meet her. She was fancied up, her face painted. Ruthie hadn't ever seen that kind of woman. Her ma didn't use such things, didn't need color plastered to her face to make her beautiful, at least not to Ruthie's eyes.

The woman yelled at Ruthie, telling her to hurry and get on with the story because she had things to do.

"Ma'am." It was a hard word that stuck in her throat, but Ruthie needed to be polite, so she tried again. "You got a husband and a horse missing?" There was no other way but to ask a question, because the woman was fiddling with the roan's bridle reins and it was making Ruthie nervous.

The question caused the woman to jerk on a single rein, and the Appaloosa threw his head, almost knocking her down. Ruthie wanted to laugh but she knew the errand was too serious for foolishness.

"We got your mister at our cabin, I think, and that black horse . . . he got knocked down, so your mister, he broke his leg and wants you to come to him." She was making up some of what she was saying. Old man Carpenter had never asked to see his wife, but Ruthie knew from listening to her ma that women wanted to know they were useful. Although, looking at the woman—all painted and dressed up in fancy clothes—she couldn't see how a man would need her for much except the bed part. Ruthie knew about the bed part, not what they did exactly, but that her ma and a man seemed to like rolling over each other. She guessed if her ma had married to have these rolling matches, well, then Mr. Carpenter, he could do the same, except why with a woman so bound up she could hardly walk, never mind ride a horse. It would take a wagon and team to get her to the cabin. And Ruthie told the woman just that. "You'll be needing a team and wagon to get you there. The Heber cabin. Best ask one of the ranch men to help." Then she nodded at the woman whose mouth hung open so that Ruthie could see black places between the teeth. She knew the woman's breath would smell.

Roany was happy to leave, swinging his big head back and sideways so that the woman had to step back and didn't have time to tell Ruthie off, or talk about her plans. If she was coming to the cabin, Ruthie thought, well, then let the ranch hands harness the team and show her the way.

Brat! How dare the child, sitting up there on a bone-yard horse, tell the wife of a man who bred only the finest stock what to do with his animals. Nasty child, but, then again, her mother was too loose and free with her affections. Rose Carpenter had worked saloons and such, but she had never considered herself a street whore.

Now she knew where Haydock was—laid up, and taking rest in that Heber woman's home. Rose would not allow her husband to remain in a filthy cabin where manners weren't taught, which was how she envisioned any home run by the likes of Maggie Heber. It was necessary to get Haydock home. She would demand that Rogelio carry out her wishes. She would see to it the wagon was drawn by their best team, the bed lined with blankets and quilts from the house, and the best brandy available to help Haydock deal with whatever pain might come from the journey.

She expected a refusal from Rogelio, and, when he said no, she quite literally stamped her foot and told the man in the most colorful language— words she did not use lightly—that his no wasn't worth a pile of shit, that he was indeed the bastard son of a Chihuahua whore and worth less than what his mother had gotten paid.

His few words were spoken between her outbursts.

"You would know, *Señora* Carpenter, exactly the value of a *peso* or a silver dollar paid for a woman's flesh."

Then Arcy appeared, his horse sweated, the boy himself dusty and scared. He did not ride to Rose, the *señora* of the great ranch, but to Rogelio, who turned his head away from the boss' wife, and then walked to the boy's horse. Arcy leaned down, speaking quickly in that infernal tongue that Rose hated and couldn't understand.

When Rogelio returned to his interrupted discussion with the *señora*, he was brief. "Arcy has seen your husband, *señora*. He is the Heber place as the child told you. Arcy did not say so, but I feel that your husband is injured more seriously than the child understood. We must see to him, and quickly."

Rose retreated to the house, where she changed to clothing more suitable for her errand of mercy. When she came back to the corrals, she and Rogelio had another confrontation. He had harnessed two draft mules to the wagon, not at all suitable for Haydock's removal from that woman's house—awkward ungainly creatures, one brown with a straggly black tail and an unruly mane, the other a reddish color with a white belly and freckles along its neck.

"They don't match, Rogelio . . . what are you thinking? He needs a good team, not this collection of misfits."

The man was not bothered by her tone of voice or the implied stupidity in his choice of animals. Rogelio's voice was slow, deliberate, and the tone, this time, truly offended Rose. "They *are* his best team, *señora*. Perhaps not in color, but they work together and their pull is easy, smooth. No stops and jerks like the blacks you prefer. They will bring *Señor* Haydock home in some comfort. He would choose this team if it was up to him."

She studied his face, gauging how far she could push. There was steel in the returned gaze, a refusal ready on the thinned mouth beneath its mustached covering.

"I want the team of blacks. Haydock likes their fancy stepping. He needn't feel like a beggar or a plowman coming home."

Rose stood in some discomfort as he unhitched the poor team while speaking in his language to the men who caught up the blacks and readied them. It took a half hour to make the exchange, and Rose knew she would make her complaint well known to Haydock after they got him home. This delay was unreasonable and she was suitably furious.

"Help me into the wagon," she commanded. "Now."

Rogelio offered his arm and she pushed herself up into the wagon seat. Then, as she reached for the lines, Rogelio's hands were faster. The team stepped up into their collars unevenly, and the wagon lurched forward, all the while Rogelio talking softly to the handsome blacks. Rose watched Rogelio's hands and fingers as they guided the blacks into a working team. She decided to be quiet and let a man do his work.

Go on faith, she told herself. *Haydock trusts this man, so it would be his wish.*

Maggie's voice was powerful when she was challenged, so Burn found it necessary to go down to the barn as she lectured her sons, giving them no mercy, caring nothing about their pride.

"You boys have been out hunting these past few days and haven't found us nothing to eat. So stop your hollering and learn to hunt . . . move slow . . . don't scare half the game in the territory by your foolishness. Bring home supper. I'm tired of either Mister English doing your work for you, or just eating roasted potatoes and greens. Now get! And don't shoot at any more strangers that ain't done nothing to you . . . yet."

Burn wouldn't want to be one of her sons, or her man for that matter, if she took it to scold him. In the barn, he made a great show of studying the mare, and, when the boys stomped past, he didn't look at them, but their curses were meant to be heard.

"God damn' smart-mouth son-of-a-bitch getting our own ma turned on us 'cause he shot a measly god-damn' bird or two!"

It came to Burn to remind them that all he had done was to have shot and actually hit something, but he knew any words from him would only make the boys angrier. He could remember being their age, although it took some hard thinking to go back that far. He had had no family then. He had been a feisty, angry seventeen-year-old wanting no man to tell him what to do. In retrospect, he was amazed that he had survived—some luck, some good sense, mostly pure stubbornness, and hunger had gotten him through those bad days.

If a man didn't have a woman to grow a garden and cook for him, he grew used to being quiet, learning how to wait, to hold his breath, to see what barely moved, to feel a soft wind, to hear a step, to watch grass bend against itself. Then he would know, without knowing, that what moved ahead was his to kill.

He'd killed too early, men who'd tormented him, shot him, stolen his horses. They thought he was a child without ever having taken a good look. One of the best lessons of his life had been learning not to judge by looks, to wait and feel the heart of any man, or woman, and not to see something pretty or weaker or smaller and figure it was easy pickings.

Those boys, Tad and Jonas, they'd not heard her words, nor would they listen if he put in his piece. They had their ma to take care of them, to make their mistakes right, to direct them when they got off course. Doing would impress these boys, doing and not lecturing on it, telling them with and without words they weren't men yet.

He watched them climb the ridge at a diagonal, pushing and shoving at each other, their laughter clear on the slow-moving air. Burn shook his head and the mare nipped at him through the rails. He had other things to tend to.

Tugging, Burn wrapped the end of the bandage around the mare's leg. Beauty snipped at his hair, pulled back. Burn grinned. It was her way of saying the leg was healing and that she wanted to get going. Beauty had had enough of the stall or getting turned out into the poorly cleaned pen. She was her sire's daughter, ready to go and keep going, wanting to find out what lay on the other side of any mountain, hill, stream, or distant flat plain. But she was wrong. A horse couldn't know the truth. The hide was delicate still, flesh slowly moving in to fill gaps, no blood though, just a tenderness that couldn't take much running, or the burden of a rider and gear.

Burn stood, rubbed the mare's muzzle, and saw the girl coming toward the pens on that Appaloosa monster. *Ah, hell,* he thought, *I can't answer no more questions.* Then came the memory of Katherine's voice, clear and soft, telling him to pay attention to how he spoke with the children. That he should know better than to dismiss them because they were curious. She had often chastised him for pretending to talk as if he had had no schooling. Sometimes he would grin at her and she would flare up even more, saying—"No nonsense . . . no fooling with the children's ability to learn." The lesson had never stuck. Her fury couldn't hold, and she'd laugh.

The child was coming toward him, grinning and climbing down from the Appaloosa whose lower lip flapped and long ears swiveled. Katherine receded in his memory. Another family, another woman—the wrong woman—but then again he was the wrong man.

"Ma says to come to the house," Ruthie announced.

Burn shook his head. "Little girl, don't you speak to a man like that."

She stopped. The Appaloosa bumped into her. "It's what Ma says . . . I'm just repeating the words."

He got into a staring contest with the girl until the Appaloosa gelding pushed her forward and she stumbled, losing the reins. The big Appaloosa carefully picked up his feet and stepped over her fallen body and walked sedately past Burn to stand next to the mare, its ungainly head turning to avoid stepping on the trailing reins.

Burn walked over to the girl, in no hurry, and, with one hand, picked her up and set her on the ground. "Your ma said that . . . well, now, to keep you out of trouble, I'll go on your word, but just this once."

She spoke right up. "Ma asked for you. Me, I'm going to put up Roany, make sure he's got a clean pen and water, and some of that hay."

He could feel her anger as he walked toward the house. He didn't blame the mite. She was big enough to ride by herself, smart enough to see what went on inside the house with the old man, even with her brothers, and Burn had no cause to tease her. He knew being told what to do always rankled. It was like riding a colt. You didn't demand, you asked and suggested and waited while the colt figured out that doing was usually easier than arguing with a lump of muscle sitting on his back.

He looked back once and saw Ruthie standing, arms crossed, face set. When she realized he was in turn watching her, she picked up the reins to the Appaloosa and marched toward the pen. Burn grinned, went on about his errand heading to the cabin.

Ruthie's cry surprised him. Burn bolted toward the sound.

From the cabin came Maggie's high-pitched voice. "What's happened? Ruthie!"

The child kept yelling: "He's dead! He's dead!"

Behind the barn, near the last pen, Ruthie's eyes sought out Burn. He couldn't see any blood on her and the Appaloosa looked all right. Burn continued toward her, trying to see what she was pointing at.

Then he saw that the black colt lay flat, gut shot, the dirt around him a darker red, flies *buzzing* about even though the air was chilly. Its teeth were bared, its tongue hanging out, and signs of thrashing showed in the churned dirt.

Burn came closer to inspect the colt. One bullet. A bad-luck shot. Then he remembered Tad's rifle having gone off unexpectedly. Everyone had breathed a sigh of relief when no one had been hit. Except there had been. The young black colt, that was now nothing but meat and hide.

The death frightened Burn because he'd been working near the corpse, and none of his senses had picked up on what had happened. Another instinct lost. God dammit.

Standing there, Burn heard the *squeal* of a dried axle, a harness *jingle,* a whip *crack* followed by a "Whoa!" He shook his head, fearing what would greet him as he turned. Ruthie flew past him, heading toward the cabin and her mother's arms.

Sure enough, a fancy, painted wagon, but its wheel *squealed* just the same. The noise bothered the off black who kept shaking his head, putting an extra half-kick step into his poor attempt at pulling. The near black was sturdier and must have been deaf, for he pulled, head held tightly against the fool overcheck. It was a sorry team even if they matched in color, right down to their hind socks and a half star between the eyes.

A *vaquero* was driving, his dark face set, his eyes straight ahead. Burn watched his hands, saw the slightest movement soothe the skittery black while trying to encourage the soured near horse. It was a masterpiece of driving and Burn appreciated it.

The team was brought to a steady, even halt, no lurching forward, no extra step. The man knew his horses, could feel what wasn't right through the reins and make adjustments. Burn was surely impressed. He stepped up to the wagon, where he could directly view the man, and then he nodded. The driver's answer was a brief smile, a similar nod.

The woman next to him in the wagon, however, began snapping as soon as Maggie appeared at the cabin door. A rough voice, using words no decent woman should know or ever use. Maggie took one step back, and Burn could see her push Ruthie inside, whispering something to the child.

As the team stood squarely, the woman gathered

up her skirts, glaring at Burn, expecting him to offer his hand. Standing only a few feet from her, he refused, shaking his head. He would not be part of this woman's world. She might be Haydock Carpenter's wife, but she wasn't a lady.

The woman settled back onto the carriage seat. "You get Haydock out here right now! I don't want him staying with her a minute longer! You have no right to keep my husband when he needs me to take care of him!"

At the cabin door, Maggie's skin was red, her eyes wide. Burn glanced at her, then moved a step toward the carriage and the raging woman and slammed his hand on the side of the fancy wood. "Ma'am, you don't talk that way 'round here," he said. He caught the look on the driver's face—a smug set to the mouth, another hint of that peculiar nod. The woman shut up, which surprised Burn.

It was the *vaquero* who spoke next, using a voice that made listening a pleasure compared to the woman. "*Señor*, we are here to inquire as to the health and whereabouts of *Señor* Carpenter. You are the one to ask?" The driver had asked Burn, man to man, which made Burn smile.

"The lady of the house knows best about Mister Carpenter," Burn responded. "She's been tending him. He has a broken leg, and there seems to be more troubling him that I don't understand. . . ."

Rose Carpenter said nothing, but she glared

first at her husband's long-time hand, and then at Burn. Both men ignored her, and Maggie had quickly removed herself inside the house where, among the shadows, she could not be seen but could hear.

"My name is Rogelio Vigil, *señor*," the driver said.

"Burn English."

Rogelio's eyes looked puzzled, then widened.

"Yes, English," Burn said.

They grinned at each other.

"I lost much money, *señor*," Carpenter's man said. "Who could know a local horse would run with such heart."

"*Senor*," Burn said, "you know horses. Why didn't you take a long look at that bay colt, instead of believing what you were told in a book or on a piece of paper? It was there for you to see . . . in his lines, his eyes, his eagerness. A horseman such as you. . . ."

Rogelio laughed. "Yes, it was a mistake. I trusted the *señor* when he said his imported stallion was unbeatable. He has a way with him . . . to make you believe."

At this point, Mrs. Carpenter began again. "I don't know what the hell you're talking about, but I want it to stop. I want my husband now! We've got blankets and straw in the wagon, so he can come home with me."

Both men stared at the woman. In the quiet,

Maggie stepped out of the cabin and approached the rig. "Missus Carpenter"—her voice carried all the worries and stress of the last day—"your husband is resting quietly. I'm sure you understand a journey to your home might. . . ." She paused, and Burn sensed how difficult this was for her. "Such a trip would kill him," Maggie finally got out.

The level of Rose Carpenter's voice went up a notch: "He is my husband and I know best!"

"Missus Carpenter," Maggie began again, "please step down and come in." Her few words were gracious, hiding how she felt and what she really wanted to add: "And see for yourself."

With the smallest of pleading looks from Maggie, Burn stepped to the wagon and offered his arm. The woman shot him a dark look, but with her wide skirts and tight corset she could not manage to climb from the vehicle on her own. He caught her weight, was surprised by her bulk, the stiffness of her body under her clothing. She pushed at him as he backed away as if he had touched her in an offensive manner.

"That's enough," she said.

Burn was amused as she went to the cabin, knowing that beneath all the geegaws and fluff was a will of iron. He wasn't looking forward to the battle that would be waged once inside. He looked at Rogelio, observing the same concern in his eyes. He couldn't help but grin as the driver nodded his head. They both knew.

CHAPTER TWELVE

Mrs. Carpenter sat there, having swept past Maggie, saying nothing and plunking herself down in the straight-backed chair where usually either Maggie or Burn sat to tend the injured man.

What is wrong with her? Can't she see how poorly her husband is doing? Maggie thought, anticipating disaster. The chair groaned under the weight of the woman and Maggie feared it would give way. If it did break, Maggie knew Mrs. Carpenter would take it as a great insult and have something more to complain about.

The woman's voice was heavy as molasses now as she talked nonsense to a man who most likely couldn't hear her. "Now, darlin', we'll have you home in no time where I can take care of you in much finer conditions. We'll set up a bed in the front parlor. You'll love looking out the window to see the mountains. Just think, though, if you'd already built that house in Salt Valley . . . why the view would be spectacular."

Maggie shook her head, wanting to slap some fool sense into the woman. Old man Carpenter rolled his head on the mound of pillows and Maggie could read the words his mouth formed, plain as day: "Stayin' right here."

His wife didn't see him, just talked on. Nothing from Carpenter but his wrinkled mouth forming and reforming the silent words. "Stayin' right here."

Finally Mrs. Carpenter turned, calling to Maggie: "Miss . . . I need the help of those men out there to get my husband into the wagon! Tell them to come in here now."

That was it. Maggie moved closer until she stood directly behind Mrs. Carpenter. "I am Missus Heber, if you don't mind using my correct name in my own house, Missus Carpenter. And there ain't no way you're taking this man out of here. If you move him to the wagon, he'll suffer terribly." She glanced briefly at Carpenter's face. He nodded as if giving her permission to continue. "That trip'll be hell on him and for no reason. He's in enough pain. So leave him be." She could see a stiffness travel through the woman's flesh—anger, hatred, maybe even fear.

Rose Carpenter's voice rose to a higher pitch. "He needs to be in his own home!" She stared at her husband while speaking, not turning to look at her opponent or acknowledging what Maggie had just said.

Maggie stayed where she could not be seen unless Mrs. Carpenter made the effort to turn around. "'Less you intend to drag him yourself, he stays here. Ain't nothing to your house can help him now. He needs quiet, good food, and no fussing."

Haydock Carpenter's drawn face attempted a grin, the corners raising just the slightest. Then his eyes closed and he was sleeping again. Sad when a simple grin wore out a man. If his wife had been paying attention, she'd see what was real and right there in front of her. Instead, the woman turned around very slowly. "You will have those men outside your place put Mister Carpenter in the wagon."

"No."

Outside, the rising pitch of Mrs. Carpenter's voice caught Burn and the driver off guard. The team stepped forward quickly, wanting to bolt from the sound. Rogelio was quick to pick up the lines, his fingers moving, his shoulders setting to halt the team. Sweat appeared on the team's necks but they were obedient to their driver.

Burn ran to the house, and bumped into Maggie who was on her way outside. They stood closer than they'd ever been, his eyes almost even with hers, seeing in their blue light a center of green and gold flecks. He saw the pleading in her gaze. He inhaled deeply, knowing that their position was too intimate, but she felt right against him and he wanted all of her.

The shrieking started again, and Burn put a hand on Maggie's forearms and moved around her, taking the few steps to the old man's bed. The woman had Carpenter by the shoulders and was screaming at him to sit up. Carpenter's face was white, his mouth hung open, his eyes were rolling back.

"You're killing him! You're killing him! My husband . . . you're killing him!" Rose Carpenter screamed.

Burn pushed his shoulder between the woman and the old man, leaned in, and felt a small puffing against his neck as he laid the frail body back. In his ear, endless and relentless, the woman's voice became louder. He slid one hand under the old man's head and slowly rested it on the pillows. Then he turned and slapped the woman, pulling back at the last moment so most of the anger he felt was in his head, not in the power of his hand.

For one blessed moment, there was no sound. Nothing. Even Ruthie, who had come over to stand near her mother, was silent. Maggie's stare held on Burn. He didn't know what to expect from either of the two woman, but then he heard a voice. Soft, small, clear.

"Thanks, son. She was hurting me," said Haydock Carpenter.

Then Rose Carpenter's hand went to her mouth and stayed there. And Maggie actually smiled.

Burn nodded and spoke to Mrs. Carpenter as if nothing unusual had just happened. "You best go home now, ma'am. Come back to visit when you can be calm. He may be yours by law, but he's here now . . . and safe . . . and we ain't letting you take him."

It finally sank in. The flounced and curled woman moved rapidly through the small cabin, what remained of her dignity pushing her through the situation.

"English." A whisper from Carpenter. "She means well, but. . . ." Then nothing more but a deep sigh.

Burn felt his heart jump, and, when he knelt down and put his ear to the old man's mouth, he could hear life holding on. He then sat in the chair.

Perhaps a half hour later, when he felt Maggie's hand on his back, he pulled away from her, the old man, the child's wide eyes as she stared at him, still quiet, terrified by the scene that had taken place in her house and that she couldn't really understand. Burn understood. He shook off the Hebers' obvious need for comforting, and went outside, drawing in the sun, the cold air, the emptiness of the yard. No horses or wagon, no driver, no harridan pretending grandness and compassion.

The mare whinnied from the corral, where only the roan Appaloosa kept her company. Burn went to her, conscious, as he walked, of the bone, the muscle, and blood holding him together, keeping him alive. His flesh remembered almost dying. And, when he looked at Carpenter, he could feel that dying, and he understood exactly what Katherine and Davey had done for him. Trying to make another human hold onto life was a rare and terrible responsibility, a difficult thing for the human soul to accept.

Mrs. Carpenter's carrying on, her pretense, her wanting her husband home as if he were suffering from a minor cut or a broken wrist was the woman's only way of dealing with the weakening body she saw lying on Maggie Heber's bed.

Burn entered the mare's pen, and went down on one knee, inhaling the warm sweet manure, the sweat, the smells of everyday life. The mare approached him and he could see the top edge of the wire cut, smooth and shiny above the dirtied bandage. The flesh was growing together so that soon enough the edges would meet and form a stronger bond. The mare lowered her head and snorted at him. Burn looked up into the opened curled edges of her nostrils, widened to take in his scent. Beauty nickered and nudged the front of his hat, pulling it off so that it dropped in a fresh pile of manure. Burn laughed. The mare stepped back, and then pushed her muzzle against his naked face. Her whiskers brushed into Burn's eyes, his mouth, and he could taste horse. Salt. Sweet. Dirt. Life.

"It won't last you know," Maggie's voice said

behind him. "She has to bring him home now. She has to show everyone that she's in command . . . not him, and especially not me. Or you."

Burn shifted the bandage, pretending preoccupation, unwilling to share his fear at what he'd felt when holding the old man or hitting the woman. It had been a crude need to shut the woman's mouth. He still felt all those sensations: human flesh under the bone of his hand, the pain, the crack on solid skin. If he raised his hand, he could smell Rose Carpenter's peculiar female odor even through the manure now coating his fingers. He studied those trembling fingers. They'd hit a woman.

"I don't know what she's thinking," Maggie began again. "One look at Mister Carpenter and the truth is easy to see. He's. . . ." She stopped, unwilling to speak the word she associated in her mind with Carpenter when she looked at him. Death.

Burn rose, using the mare's neck and withers for support. Beauty rubbed her head along his ribs, almost pushing him over.

"Ma'am," he began, "she'll be back with more of Carpenter's men, all primed to rescue their boss on the missus' say-so."

Maggie stared at him briefly before responding. "She can't do that. She's seen him . . . even touched him. How could she . . . ?"

Burn wanted to tell her what she already knew.

What he'd felt from the old man. What those tired reddened eyes held. What Ruthie was so scared of. What made Mrs. Carpenter so downright terrified and terrifying to others. It was one thing. A death coming to them, not wanted, not prepared for, not part of what Haydock Carpenter had planned for this end of his living, but visible, nonetheless. That padded and corseted and painted woman was his, by God, and he wanted more of her, on his terms, until he was too old to climb the mountain, and then he could die. Not because some sour-headed bronco had had plans of his own.

"She will come back, ma'am," he told her again. Then he took a leap, adding: "Maggie."

She had turned away from him, looking along the thin wagon road as if the wagon was already returning. But, at the sound of her name, she turned on her boot heel and faced him. Her eyes seemed to glow and Burn knew, if she asked him anything right now, he would become the fool he felt he'd always been.

"Burn. I've been waiting. Am I wrong?" She stepped in closer.

He swallowed hard. "Maggie. . . . No, you're right, even though I tried not to . . . but back there, when she was trying to make him sit up . . . you showed me."

Maggie stepped back, and again Burn remembered slapping Mrs. Carpenter. He knew that it didn't sit right with Maggie and that she needed to understand the why. "He had to be protected," Burn began. "She had to be stopped. No other way . . . and I saw you."

Then Maggie was speaking. "I saw you hold back. In that last moment, when I thought you wanted to kill her . . . and you slapped her . . . I saw you dig in and hold onto your strength. You even bit yourself in the doing." She reached out one finger and touched a cut on his lip that he hadn't even realized was there.

Neither said anything for several seconds, but then from a distance came a yell: "Ma! Ma!"

Burn put his hand on Maggie's arm. "Your boys. Be damned glad they weren't here a few minutes ago."

She looked at him. "How will I get them to go if the Carpenter men come back? Oh, Lord, Burn, I can't lose them."

He was out of his mind, but he kissed her on the mouth gently, and she kissed him back just as gently. When they pulled apart, she licked her lips. "Your blood . . . you." She headed for the cabin as Burn went to the pen that housed the dead black colt.

The boys were running toward the house. Jonas held a brace of prairie chickens high overhead. Below him, high on the ridge, he could see wheel ridges and prints of horses that made him wonder.

He knew they didn't use the old wagon, didn't have a team, and they sure didn't have visitors much.

He hoped the folks, whoever they were, weren't staying on, because the brace of prairie chickens he'd got, and the one goose Tad had managed to hit, wouldn't go far with too many people. He knew he'd have to pick shot out of the birds, which didn't leave much flesh, but he was glad he hadn't come home empty-handed. Supper would be punctuated by the *ping* of folks spitting out lead shot into the pewter bowl Ma liked so much. It had belonged to her own grandma she had told the children, as well as: "Don't you two boys take it outside for target practice or nothing like that."

Tad came up alongside Jonas. "What's going on over there? Hell, it looks like that black colt's dead. A waste o' good horse flesh. Who the hell killed him?"

They skidded sideways down the ridge, noting exactly where that English fellow was fussing around the dead colt. They crossed behind the cabin and went in the front door from the far side, not wanting to get caught up in whatever that devil-hearted man had in mind.

Burn needed a horse stronger than Ruthie's Appaloosa to get the carcass out of the corral and down to an arroyo that ran south of the cabin. The corpse needed to be far enough away to keep the coyotes and the stink away from the cabin. He figured the task would have to fall to the mare, having quickly dismissed a fleeting notion of using the cow. She wouldn't pull, not like a good ox or mule. Burn didn't like the idea of using Beauty, but already, hiding in the air, was that smell of death, and the day was warming up. He knew the smell would get stronger. He had to get the corpse moved.

As he headed toward the barn, it occurred to him he needed to tell the old man since it was his horse. So Burn went to the pump and washed his hands, feeling the water's chill work an ache deep into his bones. Then he stuck his head under the flow of water and scrubbed his face and hands.

At the cabin, he knocked before entering. On the table were a pile of feathers and three plump bird carcasses. Burn grinned. These he wouldn't have to pluck and gut. There was no one in the house. It made him curious, but it gave him time to tell the old man privately.

He stopped near the bed, cleared his throat, and heard a grunt from behind the curtain. Pulling it back, he rehearsed what he would say, but found there was no easy way to tell Carpenter. The empty chair sat in a line of sun. Dust whirled in small circles from the shifting of the curtain. He noticed for the first time that the wood on which it hung was dried out and the pegs were coming loose at the back. He'd have to fix that he thought to himself as he shifted the chair.

The old man still had life. He grinned, not much, but enough. "She's hell on wheels," he said a little above a whisper.

Burn grunted, uncertain which woman Carpenter was insulting—or complimenting.

Carpenter rolled his head. "Both of them going at each other." He stopped, his hands bunched up on the quilt, his face greasy. "Don't like seeing fight in a woman, but there's times. . . . Rose, now, she don't always use much sense. Can't blame her. Her life's not been an easy ride."

Burn sat down, swiping at the agitated dust, still looking out the grimed window to see light and air and freedom. Death was on his mind, inside his whole body now—too much death and no words to tell it.

"Boy." Short breaths. A clawed hand scratching on the quilt. "You got something to tell me. I can see it."

Burn continued to stare out the window, determined not to look at the old man. "In the dust-up this morning, one of your hands, a boy, come in to see you. To find you." His gaze wavered, then he quickly glanced again at Carpenter, who was licking his lips, eyes closed, head turned blindly toward Burn on the pillows. "Maggie's boys," Burn began again, realizing it wasn't right to be speaking her name so casually.

"Tad and Jonas, they got excited. They meant to shoot at your man to scare him. No one got hurt."

"But?" Carpenter said.

Burn thought the old man was stronger than he was himself. Carpenter already knew somehow and he was being kind, letting Burn stumble through. "Shot killed your black," he managed to get out. He waited, then heard those short breaths again before saying: "Sorry. They didn't mean to . . . had the rifle loaded and it got dropped."

"Weren't much of a horse. Pretty color, though, that the missus liked." More labored breathing.

Burn watched a chicken hurry across the yard, chased by an overhead shadow. *Another thing to do,* he thought. *Need to build her a better coop or the hawks'll be eating chicken for breakfast.*

"Bet Rogelio got roped into driving them damned blacks," Carpenter said. "She . . . she thinks they're smart. My weakness, boy. Kept that colt uncut too long." A shaky pause. Then: "Vanity does strange things, a man gets older."

Burn spoke, wanting to give the old man a rest. "I'll drag out the body. Need to get it from the pens . . . but I thought, well . . . you needed to know first. Maybe you got something else in mind for the colt."

"Hide'd make a good rug," Carpenter said. "Pretty . . . that black color, but the sun'll hit it inside the house and it'll go green." A grin passed over his face.

Burn laughed and asked: "Pair of chaps, then?"

"Don't think Rose'll be using chaps. She prefers them fancy steppers of hers. But you can make yourself a pair, you have the mind to." Then a pause and a wicked smile. "Can't see that behind of hers in black chaps against them wide-ended britches she'd have to wear."

Burn laughed at the image, and put his hand over his mouth, feeling his face turn red.

"You got it, boy. Ain't a real pretty picture," Carpenter said, then was quiet. His face looked frail, his eyes grew smaller, and his hands spread across the quilt, no longer moving. Burn touched the back of one hand, felt the cool skin, but the old man's chest still rose and fell. Burn hadn't been left alone.

Maggie was back in the room now, near the table, hands on her hips, staring at the three birds. Flies *buzzed* around them, hungry now that winter had disturbed their usual outdoor feasts.

"I told him 'bout the colt," Burn informed her, getting up and walking toward her. He kept the table between them. Yet even this close she was temptation.

"The boys brought in supper," she said.

"Saw them. They went 'way around me to get into the house."

She smiled, her eyes sparkling, her mouth wide, and he wanted to leap over the table. Instead, he planted his ugly hands on its surface.

She touched the back of one hand, where the worst of the scarring began. "They're terrified of you, Burn, but they listen. I don't like them taking the shotgun. We'll be spitting out lead at dinner, but at least they were able to get something this time."

"Ma'am."

She frowned.

"Maggie," he began instead, "they need to learn to shoot straight and to stalk. And they're trying." He left before he had to fight off the desire to kiss her. It wasn't the time or place. An old man dying . . . the colt's bloating flesh needing to be moved.

The mare wasn't much interested when he approached the corral with a harness, and the Appaloosa simply turned his butt toward Burn at the sound of the laying of leather and metal over the top rail.

Burn harnessed the Appaloosa first, and noted ancient gall marks on the bony shoulder and withers. At least one half of the team knew how to work in harness. When he slid the collar and hames over the mare's head and neck, she threw herself back, the white of her eyes showing. Burn talked to her, ran his hand along her neck to the flat jowl, and then to her muzzle. She lowered her head. He used her bridle, not the stiff, moldy one with blinkers, and snapped the reins onto the snaffle rings. The mare sighed and relaxed. At least the bridling was familiar, and she was safe next to the Appaloosa that took the blinkered bridle the way he accepted everything—a shake of his rat-tail, a fart, and a deep exhalation of breath.

Burn had already wrapped a well-used and dusty rope around the colt's swollen girth. It took a few tries to get the mare in step with the Appaloosa as he guided them together around the outside of the opened corral, careful to keep the mare away from the corpse of the dead colt so she wouldn't spook.

Then it was time to try halting and backing the team. The mare froze when he asked through his hands. She threw up her head and braced her front legs. It had been with his body, his legs against her side, his weight set quietly on her back, then the slightest of touch against her mouth to ask for that backward step. Now it could only be through his hands.

The Appaloosa understood and stepped back, jerking the singletree separating him from the mare. The mare shied sideways, then went back with the Appaloosa, head turned to the outside but finally in step with her teammate. He got them in between the gateposts, and slid the reins through his hands as he stepped back to hook the singletree chain onto the black's rope. It was going to get wild and woolly, but there wasn't any choice besides butchering out the colt where he lay, and for that he didn't have the stomach.

There must have been a shift in the singletree for the mare cocked her head, then jumped sideways, placing herself up against a gatepost where Burn didn't want her. The Appaloosa held his ground, guided by Burn's hand on the lines holding him steady. The mare started to fret, trotting in place, looking for an out now that she felt trapped by the Appaloosa and the post and the thing *jingling* beside her.

When she shifted away from the post and was almost in a straight line with the Appaloosa, Burn urged them both forward, loosening his hold, clucking, calling the mare's name. She jumped at the chance of freedom. The singletree chain *rattled* and tightened. The Appaloosa knew what he was being asked to do, but the mare threw her head wildly, tearing the lines from Burn's right hand and jerking herself against the Appaloosa's slow forward pull.

There was a moment when the Appaloosa pulled, then stopped, and the mare sulled, jerked forward, her body shifting, sliding a foot or two. The mare was panicking, kicking back, just missing Burn as he bent down to reach the line. He called her name, slapped the lines on the Appaloosa's bony rump. The Appaloosa went forward, with ears pinned, insulted at the scolding. The mare found her buddy in step with her and then she, too, began to pull.

As Burn hoped, the corpse turned at a sideways angle and was jerked, bouncing through the gate and out into the yard. The mare wanted to head west. The Appaloosa tried to listen to Burn. The arroyo was south of the cabin, a good half mile or more. Once he convinced the mare she could not take off on her own but was tied to the Appaloosa, they proceeded with jerks, then a breather, then more jerks and tugs until they hit a downhill slope and Burn had to hurry the team so the body didn't roll over them.

When they got to the edge of the arroyo, Burn tried to maneuver the team to the edge without the colt rolling over the lip. He was depending on the Appaloosa to hold steady as the mare fidgeted, kicking out, even whinnying a few times. At that moment he made a promise to her, like he'd promised her sire, he'd never put her in harness again.

The Appaloosa held quiet long enough so that Burn could back the team, loosening the chain and taking the risk of sliding his hand under the rope, which was pulled tight, to release the colt. A jerk now and he'd panic the mare and lose his hand or at least a finger. He was cautious, since he had gotten this far in life with all his fingers and toes and wanted to go out with all his pieces still strung together.

The *jangling* chain spooked the mare and the singletree slammed against her knee and hock and she kicked out, catching the Appaloosa in the flank, who then turned and took a good bite at her neck. Burn hurried to their heads and took both of them at the bit, tugging down, releasing, and tugging again. The two horses finally eased up and the mare even rubbed against him.

He left the rope on the colt while he pushed and kicked until the body rolled down into the arroyo. Coyotes would feast tonight. Then he unhooked the singletree, removed the hames and both collars, and had two bridle horses with leftover reins. So he swung up on the mare's back, talking to her, telling her the humiliation was over, forever forgotten, never to be repeated. She didn't believe him, and, as soon as his butt touched her back, she bogged her head, squealed, and bucked like crazy. All he could think was—*Oh, hell!*—as the third buck sent him flying. He found out then that the extra length of rein was useful, for the mare ran up against the leather's end held tightly in Burn's fist, a reflex from all those years ago, and she turned to the pull, remembering what she'd once been taught.

Through all the bucking, the Appaloosa simply cocked a hind leg and took a short nap.

CHAPTER THIRTEEN

Burn walked back leading both horses, footsore by the time he got to the cabin but rump-sore enough from the buck Beauty had given him that he'd chosen the lesser pain. Either way his pride had taken its usual beating. He was getting too old.

The boys were at the cabin door, cleaning their shotgun and squabbling. They were laughing by the time Burn finished unharnessing the unlikely team. He moved slowly, feeling a rub across his hip when he moved. *Damn*. He took extra time with the mare, being slow and careful in removing the bridle while keeping one rein tied around her neck. She needed his attention now to remind her that their partnership hadn't fallen apart.

He brushed her, scrubbed her neck, especially where the heavy collar and hames had scuffed the hair. She seemed to forgive him, once again rubbing her head on his arm and taking a bite of his coat, holding the thick canvas in her mouth.

He left her alone in the pen and tended to the Appaloosa, who needed the same cleaning up but not the affection. He fed out hay even though it was still light, not suppertime, and then he limped up to the cabin, figuring to make a stop at the pump and remove the muck and filth he'd gotten into. It was the sounds that haunted him more than any of the afternoon's actual efforts—the thickness of heavy flesh slamming, rolling, dragging. Flesh become meat, without soul or heart.

He took off his coat, glanced at the sleeve, and saw the wet uneven circle where the mare had taken hold of the canvas. He was grinning even as he pumped the chilled water over his hands.

The boys were seated on the front steps, watching, silent now. The shotgun lay across their laps, barrel resting on one set of thighs, stock on the other. Burn shrugged back into his coat, shook his head, ran fingers through the mat of his hair, and slammed his hat back on. He walked to within two feet of the boys, who would not look up at him but studied the shotgun. Whether a threat or a distraction, Burn didn't care.

He said: "You killed that colt and I took care of the body. Now you go get the collars and hames, the singletree, and bring 'em home. Clean up that harness and store it decent, in the barn. You might not have a team, but there's no call to let equipment go to hell for want of hard work and some oil."

Jonas stood up, grabbing the butt end of the shotgun. There wasn't enough room to swing the barrel around, which was how Burn had planned it.

"Careful now. That's how you killed Mister Carpenter's fine black horse only you had a rifle then," Burn said as he shoved the barrel away from its position close to his belly. "You boys, clean up your mess. I done the worse part of the dirty work for you."

Maggie was at the door, and she sealed the deal, telling the boys: "You do what Burn tells you . . . *now*. He knows, and you don't."

Burn's hand didn't quiver as he slid the shotgun out of the boys' hands and moved toward the cabin door. He turned back toward the boys. "I drug that colt south to the wash. You can't miss those tracks. Gear got left waiting right there. I didn't want to burden the mare with more work. She ain't ready for it." He couldn't help blaming the boys for their idiotic behavior that had caused the death. "You go get that harness and such. Then hang it right in the barn like I told you."

He was aware that Maggie's head was nodding so the boys couldn't dare object. It was probably more than he needed to say, but the boys were young enough that they needed instructions to be repeated several times to sink in.

A howl drew the attention of all four, followed by another.

Burn looked at Maggie. "They already got to the colt," she said.

Ruthie came outside, stepping in close to her mother and grabbing onto her skirt. She looked up into Maggie's face. "Are they going to hurt Roany," she asked, "and the mare, too? What about our chickens, Mama? How can they be safe?"

The boys returned in about a half hour. It seemed to Burn that the entire day had been taken up with that one chore. Now here were the boys, laughing and punching at each other, unaffected by what had had to be done about the colt. He asked them questions, but they didn't answer until Maggie told them to show some respect.

Finally Jonas said: "Yep . . . them coyotes got right to the colt." Then he began a detailed description about what they'd seen. Ruthie was setting the supper table, and it was easy to see that she was listening and taking in everything that her brothers were saying.

Burn laid a hand on the boys' shoulders and pressed down, smiling at them, but deliberately trying to cause pain. The boys stopped their talk, whining and wiggling, but they didn't try to get away from him. "That's enough," he said.

Maggie told them to get more firewood, which was their chore, reminding them they had not been keeping the woodbox filled.

Jonas headed outside. Tad opened his mouth to complain, but Burn grabbed his forearm. The boy said—"Yes, Ma."—and went out.

Burn looked at Maggie, who was smiling. "They ain't bad boys, Mister English."

He winced. "Burn," he reminded her.

They both smiled, kind of foolish and kind of sweet. The boys brought in wood. The *clunk* and *clatter* broke the small moment between them.

There was little conversation at supper. The only sounds were the *ring* as any piece of shot found by the diners was spit into the bowl set in the middle of the table, and the occasional coyote howl. With each howl everyone would stop chewing as their eyes widened and their heads turned toward the distant sound. They all knew what it meant.

Burn was worried about Ruthie, who ate only tiny bits of the tasty game bird, and some of her turnip, a bite of carrot. She kept herself close to her ma and flinched at the sound of every howl. Burn had a glimpse into the world of parent and child, for Maggie's face mirrored her daughter's fear.

The dark was thick on this moonless night when Burn checked on the mare and the roan. He'd bedded them in the barn, and even then the mare was shivering, and it wasn't that cold. Like Ruthie, she seemed to be made nervous by the echoing howls that announced the animals' triumphant find. He fed out extra hay, then returned to the house.

The old man was half sitting up. His face was pale but there was a new spark in his eyes. "They sure do talk, don't they?" he said. "Kinda like them women that come to the house to knit or something. All talk . . . nothing but. . . ." His voice faded but he had given Burn a glimpse of what Carpenter had put up with in his past.

Burn took the broth bowl from the stove and picked up a big-handled spoon carved out of one piece of wood, well-made and easy to hold. He sat in the chair by the bed and held the bowl as the old man managed two or three dips of the soup. He even picked out the few bits of meat and got them into his mouth. He pushed the meat around, drool showing at the corners of his mouth, but then he swallowed and grinned, and unexpectedly Burn was pleased.

"She's a good woman," Carpenter said.

Burn looked at him, puzzled, and the old man grinned.

"Her . . . the one you're set on . . . not Rose. I married her 'cause I was lonesome and she'd put up with me fumbling over her."

Burn jerked, and broth spilled from the mug.

"Don't mean it dirty, boy. Mean it to be the truth."

Burn said nothing as he dabbed at the spill with a rag he'd brought from the table to use as a napkin.

"She's taken with you, boy. Don't know why. You ain't much to look at. Now don't get in a hissy, but I'm sure you heard this before. Can't

195

tell me no man's ever called you on your size."

Burn tried to keep his face blank as he stared at Haydock Carpenter.

"That's what I mean, boy. You know 'xactly who you are and I admire you for it. Hell, your rep' with them horses you bred is all a man really needs in his life. That, and a good woman. I'm betting you been lonesome too long. Most of your life maybe, or you'd see what that woman standing behind you is thinking."

Burn shifted around on the chair and there was Maggie, one hand on her daughter's neck, rubbing and giving comfort, while her eyes smiled at the old man's blunt words and Burn's confusion. When he turned back to Carpenter, wanting to get the feeding over with, the man was still sitting up, but sound asleep. It took a few moments, a bit of gentle handling, before he was able to slide the old man into a prone position, head propped on the pillow, leg raised up on a mound of blankets. Carpenter snored through the repositioning.

Maggie helped Ruthie take the half-empty broth bowl and pour the soup back into the pot. She then rinsed out the bowl with a small amount of water.

Ruthie said: "Mama, he's getting better. He talks more and I can make sense of what he says." Then she studied on the thought; "Most of it anyway."

A coyote howled and the child jerked. Maggie held her, looking over her head at Burn.

He nodded, decided to go outside, hauling a jacket with him and shucking into it as he went to the woodpile. There were rocks scattered near the barn, so he dumped an armful of wood near them and hunkered down. He was careful to fit the rocks in a circle, making sure each was situated firmly. It was easy to fill in with a bit of dried grass, a few thin sticks. A match against the grass flamed out quickly, caught the twigs, and there was a fire to feed.

Tad came out first. He was slow to approach, but Burn asked him to pick up a log and place it carefully on the fire, which the boy did. Then he, too, hunkered down, knees drawn up to his chest. No words. Just a nod and a smile as his hands turned out to the fire's warmth.

Jonas came out then, picking up more wood without being directed and stacking it neatly near Burn, before he squatted next to his brother. "To keep the coyotes out?" Jonas asked.

Burn only nodded.

"For Ruthie?" This was from Tad.

Burn finally smiled.

Much later Maggie came out, carrying her daughter. Burn rolled over a tall thick log so that she had somewhere to sit other than on the ground, while holding the child. Burn studied Tad as he put two fresh logs across the embers. The fire built up and licked the sky. The howls drifted away and Ruthie shifted in her mother's arms.

The fire warmed their fronts while the chilling wind worked in through gaps in their clothing—a low waistband, a thin-collared shirt. Their unbuttoned coats got fastened tightly up to the throat. No one moved other than to feed the fire. Ruthie slept deeply, no longer flinching each time a coyote howled. After a while Burn got up and stood over Maggie and the child, offering his arm to help pull them up.

Burn watched Maggie walk to the cabin, Ruthie's legs dangling almost to the ground. He saw the effort in Maggie's step to keep her child in her arms. *Too big to be carried . . . too young to be left on her own,* he thought to himself. When the cabin door was shut, Burn sat back down and took note that one of the boys had added a new log.

Tad and Burn curled up near the lowering flames, saddle blankets pulled from the barn providing warmth and safety. Jonas kept watch, fed the fire. Two hours later it was Tad's turn, followed by Burn's taking over after another two rounds of the clock. It was 3:00 in the morning by his reckoning as he laid back, watching the stars, letting the boys sleep out the night.

He was yawning and kicking one booted foot through the glowing ash when Maggie came out and handed him a cup of steaming coffee. The sun was just rising as he took the tin cup that was hot to the touch, and welcome. He sipped the brew, staring at her over the cup rim. He saw her quick glance at the sleeping boys, her approval.

"You'll do, Burn English. Ain't much of you, but it's all the good stuff."

He blushed as he took another sip. "Thank you . . . for this." He lifted the cup.

She waved her arm over her two boys, saying: "For this, and for helping Ruthie last night. I don't think she would have slept at all if you hadn't started the fire watch."

He swallowed more of the hot coffee and it burned all the way down. It tasted like pine oil, the best he'd ever had.

Four Rafter JX riders came into the yard first. Their horses were lathered, their faces red from sun and anger. Neither Arcy nor Rogelio, the driver with the hands like velvet on the horses' mouths, were among the four. These were men with skills Burn recognized.

"We will have the *señor*," one announced. "Now!"

Burn looked up at the speaker. He had a broad face, deeply browned, and his dark eyes were hidden under a brimmed hat. A threat, not spoken but present, was alive between them.

"So, you plan on slinging him over the back of one of these nags you're riding and taking him home?" Burn said. "He's a dying man in no shape for that kind of stunt." He was angry at the men's stupidity. His eyes ached. He wanted to rub them, lie down, and sleep, but the horsemen had circled him and he was conscious that he had no weapon in his hand, no knife at his belt. Nothing.

A horse came close, brushed past Burn's shoulder, intending to spin him. Burn used the opportunity to climb the horse's side, grab the horse's mane and the neck of the rider, and hold on. When he fell back, he took the man with him. Both rolled on the ground, but, as they came to a halt, Burn was seated on the man's considerable belly. There was a knife in his hand now, easily taken from the rider's wide *concha* belt, and convenient for Burn's use. He touched the very tip of the knife blade to the throat that was exposed to him.

He found the remnants of his rough Spanish. "You will not take the old man. He will die from your pride." The knife tip pricked skin, drawing one large blood bead. As the man swallowed, mouth flooding with fear, the blood drop rolled in a reddish thread across the man's skin, sticking in the wrinkles, veins, and dark hairs. Burn pulled himself away and up, spinning slowly, the knife loose in his hand, but moving across his body so it could not be taken away from him.

The fallen horseman struggled to his knees. A *compadre* led the riderless horse in close as the man caught a stirrup and slid up into the saddle. That was all. The horses led off in a line, following the remounted spokesman of the group. A whirl of dust and yells followed in their wake, and curses, if Burn's poor Spanish was right. Then the small yard was quiet again.

Burn was wiping his mouth when Maggie came to him, a half-filled bucket of water in one hand. He grinned as she poured the water over his head, leaving just enough for him to have a good, healthy drink. He felt the tang of the metal rim on his lips, but it didn't matter, the water tasted just fine.

"She won't give up, will she?" Maggie asked.

"No, ma'am." Water dripped from his chin, chilling him as it rolled into his shirt and onto his skin. "Don't know what's got into that woman or the men who work for the brand. But moving him would mean pure death for Carpenter and that don't take a doctor to spell out. Any man with an ounce of sense would know that much."

When Maggie didn't say anything, Burn added what he had been thinking during his watch in the night. "There a doc nearby? A town? I'd send your girl. She can ride and has the heart. She can take the bay mare. That Appaloosa would make a two-day trip out of a three-hour journey."

"There's a doc in Mancos," she said. " 'Bout a three-hour ride on a good horse."

Burn thought about that for only a few seconds.

"Yeah . . . the mare can make that trip. Besides, your girl don't weigh much and she can use that light child's saddle."

"But the mare," Maggie said, "she's been laid off quite a while now. Won't she be too much for Ruthie?"

"Beauty's hot, that's a truth, but she's. . . ." He couldn't say it, bragging came hard to him.

She understood the source of his discomfort. "You trained her and you trust her."

He nodded, but he had to tell her the truth about Beauty. "She's a mite more horse than your girl's ever ridden. I'll not say I won't worry about her."

Maggie's hand rested briefly on his face and he leaned against the light pressure. "Thank you, Burn. But after those men . . . and their crazy desire to take him . . . we need someone with authority to tell the Carpenter woman how dangerous her idea is."

Burn smiled, feeling the ghost of her fingers still touching him. "Seems like we're maybe risking too much for the old man, who's probably going to die anyway. Maybe it's a bad idea. I'd go myself . . . but if they came back while I was gone. . . ." Maggie's face tightened as Burn kept talking. "But then again, I don't see that we have a choice. Your boys couldn't ride that mare. I don't trust their sticking to a task. I can't leave, and neither can you. And we can't have the old man die by letting him go home in a damned wagon. He deserves some better than that."

Maggie was quiet. Burn took a risk and pulled her to him, her head bowed and rested on his shoulder. He could feel the in and out of her breathing.

"Burn," she whispered into his ear, "we ain't got a choice."

He buried his face in her hair, only for a moment. She pulled him closer to her. He inhaled her—her cooking and her fear and her being a woman. She was smiling against his neck; he could feel the softest movement of her lips just below his ear.

Burn wrapped the mare's leg in a soft cloth, using more of the tar ointment on the wound. He tied off the bandage with a few wraps from an old shirt and hoped it would hold. He spent extra time brushing the mare, then bridled her, and brought her out into the yard.

Oh, hell, he thought, *one more time ain't going to kill me.* He immediately regretted his choice of words as he swung up onto the mare's back. She humped, swished her tail, and pinned back her ears, and he hadn't done anything but sit on her.

Stroking her neck, speaking sweet words under his breath softly, sort of like praying, he pressed his legs against her sides, asking her, not demanding, that she walk forward in a polite manner.

Beauty's response was predictable. She snorted, pulled the reins loose, and bucked. Nice polite forward bucks with no kicking high behind, no sideways leaps. Polite lady-like crow-hops that took them across the yard in a straight line, almost directly into Maggie who'd come out to watch. Maggie's hand was over her mouth, her eyes glowing as Beauty, with Burn still attached, made a slow circle to the left. Then, as Burn drew in lightly on the reins and used his legs against her sides, the bucks transformed into the trot the mare had inherited from her sire. Long even strides, that were so smooth a man could sit, enjoy a cup of coffee, and read the morning paper if he had a mind to.

"Burn, you're out of your mind!" Maggie called out, smiling.

Burn tipped his head and said: "Yes, ma'am, just thought I'd test her out. She's gonna be fine. Your Ruthie, she's got her a light hand and that's all it takes for Beauty to ride real gentle."

He slid down, landed near Beauty's injured leg, and squatted down to check if the bandage had stayed in place. His hands searched, straightening the wrap. Maggie had moved behind him. He didn't need to turn and look; he could smell her, taste her, feel her hand touch his shoulder. Nothing was like how he felt with her close.

"Will it hold?" she asked.

"I'll give Ruthie more wraps to use as bandages in the saddlebags. She'll need to take a rest, check the leg. But it'll be fine," he assured her.

He did not let her know his concerns or that he felt as though he was sacrificing his horse for the cause of the dying old man. Strangely he felt no anger; in fact, he laughed as he stood up. Short and compact, those strong, scarred hands were gentle on Beauty's face as the mare rubbed against his arm. He cupped her muzzle, played his fingers against her lips until the mare opened her mouth and took hold of one knuckle. Horse and man held each other. Maggie was unaccustomed to seeing such a connection, as she observed that the mare did not bite, the man did not shove.

"She's a good one, Maggie. Ruthie'll do just fine."

Whatever had driven Burn English from his past, Maggie knew he was a gift for her and Ruthie. And the boys, if they would accept him.

The child's saddle was weightless as he lifted and placed it on the doubled blankets. The cinch wasn't long enough, so he used his own, which allowed the latigo to be drawn up and tightened. He'd have to show Ruthie how to check from the saddle. Beauty liked to hold her breath in the beginning, and, down the line, a loosened cinch could cause a wreck.

"I know that already, Mister English," Ruthie said when he advised her. "I know horses blow up, and I always check. I've been riding for years."

He didn't laugh at her adult statement, figuring she was telling the truth. He knew she'd ridden the Appaloosa for at least five years. So he watched the child walk up to the side of Beauty, put her hand, palm up, fingers flattened, to the mare's muzzle for a sniff and a rub. She was already tall, close to his height, but still a kid.

"All right then," Burn announced. "Here." He turned the stirrup, held the mare, and Ruthie swung up quickly, landing lightly, and took up the reins.

"It ain't a regular bit, mister. Anything different to it?"

"She neck reins. Just go light on her mouth and she's fine. Sit down, say whoa, and she stops. Rise to the trot. When she's breathing hard, give her a break. And I already told you 'bout checking the wrap."

"Yes, sir."

Chapter Fourteen

Ma was in heat again. It was that runt who showed up barely able to walk. Tad had to admit that Burn's horse was a beauty and that he wouldn't mind putting his brand on her, but the man . . . hell, Ma'd done better in the past. Big sons-of-bitches who knew how to treat a woman. But not this sorry bowlegged specimen who thought he could teach Ma's two sons how to stalk game and shoot it. Damn, but they'd been feeding their family all right till the s.o.b. showed up.

Jonas shoved Tad in the ribs as Ruthie rode off on the pretty mare, trotting out while she hung onto the saddle swell and let the mare pick her pace. Jonas knew a good run would get her there sooner. What the hell was wrong with the girl? She knew about horses; she knew how to make time.

Tad opened his mouth to call out to Ruthie, but Jonas knocked him sideways so he couldn't get his breath.

"You shut up, damn you, Tad. Ma'll get mad if we tell Ruthie how to ride. After all, it's that man's horse, not ours. Ma won't take to us talking over him."

Tad rubbed his sore ribs and looked at his brother. He saw that something else was in Jonas's eyes. A light that meant he had a plan. Tad shook his head out of habit—nothing Jonas ever planned worked.

"Listen," Jonas began, "we got to take that old man to his home. Ma'll thank us for the doing 'cause he put Ruthie to the risk of riding all that way, and you know the doctor won't be happy."

Tad thought over what Jonas said. He didn't understand all the fuss being made over the old man. Broke his leg, didn't he? That weren't much. Get him home, let him heal. So maybe Jonas had a plan that finally might work.

It was easy hitching up the roan. Since Burn English had arrived, things were clean and neat so the harness wasn't tangled up or stiff. Tad had some trouble separating the two harnesses and figuring out how to set up the hitching of one horse to the singletree, but he had an eye and got it done. The Appaloosa kept flipping his head and whinnying. Tad slapped him good, but the horse turned around and bit Tad's hand. He slapped the horse again until Jonas told him to quit it.

They lined the wagon bed with lots of straw—no sense in bouncing the old man. Again the Appaloosa began to whinny and fuss, so one of the boys had to hold him at the bridle while the other filled the bed. They fought over who would do what now, which was settled once Tad grabbed the bit and jerked on the roan's head. He glared at Jonas as if daring him.

By the time they pulled the wagon up to the cabin door, Jonas was fighting mad. Tad had a firm grip on the bridle so it was Jonas who had to go get the old man.

Before he got in the door, his ma came out, hands on her hips. "What're you boys planning?"

Jonas brushed past her. Hell, he was old enough that no woman could tell him what to do.

"Boy!" A hand grabbed his arm, spun him around.

It's that son-of-a. . . . Jonas stopped his thoughts before he could speak them out loud.

"You ain't taking that old man nowhere . . . ," Burn said as he stepped outside, still holding Jonas's arm. "In that wagon least of all. You got any sense to you, son?"

Jonas wanted to cry out that he wasn't the runt's son. He wanted his ma to tell the man to let go. English's grip hurt, and, when Jonas pulled back, staring into the horseman's face, those fingers clamped down even more. He quit struggling finally, and just stood quietly, his arm hurting like hell. Then he saw the shotgun in the man's arm and went absolutely still. Only then did Jonas realize that horses and riders were filling up the ranch yard. His mouth went dry. He was actually scared.

The noise, the voices, the telltale dust were distracting all of them. The Appaloosa whinnied and pawed and Maggie heard Tad's voice yelling at the stubborn horse.

Burn shoved Jonas back into the cabin and held Maggie back, pushing himself in front of her. He broke open the shotgun over his arm. No man could misunderstand his meaning. He was ready, but he would wait to see what played out.

It was those same four Rafter JX men on lathered, hard-breathing horses. They were followed by Rogelio in the wagon, eyes looking down, away from Mrs. Carpenter, who was perched next to him. Even the boy was there— Arcy—on a different horse this time.

Rose Carpenter's face displayed the same high tone of the brick-red dress she wore. She directed her first words at Burn English.

"There's too many of us now, whoever you are! I want my husband, and a broke shotgun won't stop me. Besides, you ain't man enough to shoot a woman." As she spoke, she climbed down from the wagon, catching her thick skirt on the end of the doubletree. She reached behind her and yanked at the ruffle, which tore. Not one of the men in her husband's employ made any effort to help her. She only stopped at the sound of the *clicking* into place of shotgun barrels.

Burn spoke clearly. "I can draw back on the hammers, ma'am . . . if you need that much encouragement. I ain't shy 'bout shooting fools."

Outrageous, thought Rose Carpenter. *Never would a true gentleman speak to a lady in such a manner.* Still she froze, glaring at her husband's defender. It was absurd.

"You don't scare me, sir. You will put that foolish weapon down and stand aside." Then all the questions she had been asking herself came out without hesitation. "Why do you care what happens to my husband? Are you the person who injured him? What makes him so important to you?"

She thought her words would disarm the man, yet, when she took a step, he cocked one hammer. Now it was up to her.

Maggie drew in a quick breath as she studied the side of Burn's face. He was serious, and, if she were in Rose Carpenter's shoes, she would study those eyes, flashing now, a brilliance unfamiliar to her. She saw him watching the woman, without breathing, without moving, nothing indicating his thoughts except those eyes flat on the woman's face. Maggie was close enough to Mrs. Carpenter to see the rise of color, and she knew how the woman felt. She even had sympathy for Rose Carpenter with her fears. She knew what it felt like, that cold sweaty all-over sensation and a racing heart.

Rose shook her head and her mouth thinned out, making her lumpy face even more unpleasant to look at. Her intentions were clear. She took a step, taunting Burn, thinking the a man would never shoot at a woman, not in the wide open with all these witnesses.

The roar set off a number of reactions. The Appaloosa threw up his head and bolted over Tad. Rogelio's team of steady sorrels snorted and trembled, before settling back in place. And Rose Carpenter fell to her knees, hands over her ears, sobbing out indecipherable words.

The second hammer was drawn back. This time that isolated *click* held more than a threat. Burn's shot had drilled a chunk of cloth from Rose's wide-brimmed hat and sprinkled the arm of a *vaquero* reaching for his own pistol. The *vaquero* put the reins in his teeth and moved his hand over the bleeding wound as his mount spun in circles, came up against the horse of one of his *compadres*.

Everyone listened as Burn spat out his words directly at Mrs. Carpenter. "Your husband is dying . . . and it's bad. Taking him home means nothing to him. He barely knows where he is sometimes. If you want to comfort him, lady, you come sit with him, hold his hand, feed him, and wipe his bottom so Missus Heber and I don't have to do all the caring of him. Sit up through the night with him and tell him that you love him. He's your husband, ma'am. But right now he's Missus Heber's guest."

Maggie knew Carpenter's men, who faced Burn, heard the quiet conviction in his voice. No fear, no worry about what he'd just done. Only the conscience of a strong man who knew one truth. Maggie wanted to walk over and touch the back of Burn's neck. She even began to take a half step, but he shook his head, the smallest of movements, and Maggie, understanding, stood quietly.

"Ma'am." Burn's voice was stronger now. "Missus Carpenter, no one here challenges you about your husband. No one here deliberately hurt him. You want to see him?" He took a short back step and lowered the shotgun. "You go on inside with Missus Heber. You mind your manners, and she'll take you to your husband."

Harsh, Maggie thought, *and humiliating,* but she also knew that the woman was capable of almost anything. Once Mrs. Carpenter had stood up, Maggie guided her toward the house, her fingers on one hand barely touching the woman's elbow.

Burn laid the shotgun down against the firewood splitting stump, breaking it first, butt down, barrels open, harmless, yet still within reach. It was then that he noticed Tad still sitting on the ground. His head was bowed, cupped in both hands. Jonas had wandered back to the barn. *Good,* Burn thought, *that'll keep 'em out of any more trouble.* Watching the two women enter the cabin unlocked his belly, Burn let out a sigh, and just wished he could simply disappear.

Leaving the broken shotgun as a reminder, he approached the man he'd shot.

"My apologies."

The man nodded, his face set as another of the horsemen ripped at his sleeve.

"I saw you reach for your gun," Burn said, "and thought I'd make my point twice . . . with one shot."

The wounded man's face widened into a grin. "I have often thought of trying such a thing, but. . . . Congratulations, *señor*, you are a fine shot."

Burn grinned back. "Believe me, *señor*, when I tell you luck was steadying my hand."

On the wagon, Rogelio laughed. Behind him, Arcy sat on his steady bronco and held the sorrel team quiet, which did not seem to be much of a job.

"I wish to thank you," Rogelio said. "You are brave to face all of us, and to fire so accurately. I am certain Esequiel agrees that it was his actions that got him wounded. He will not hold a grudge . . . this I promise."

As for Esequiel, he looked down at Burn, stared into the worn face, searched the fading green eyes, and finally reached over the wide horn on his saddle and shook Burn's hand. Those who'd been crowding in moved back, and Burn let out a sigh, echoed by the loosening circle of men.

• • •

Inside the cabin, Mrs. Carpenter went straight to the curtained-off corner and ripped the fragile sheet back, tearing one ring through the aged fabric. Her husband lay flat, head resting on a pillow. His broken leg was elevated, a thick stack of old saddle blankets underneath. There was stink from the bed—bodily functions and infection, too. Maggie feared removing the wood splints to find out.

The woman immediately held her nose. "Haven't you been bathing him?" she asked. "Haven't you bothered to wash him after . . . well, you know?"

Maggie bit her lip. "Missus, we've been washing and emptying out his thunder mug and wiping his bottom like he's our own babe, and don't you go suggesting no different. He's sick. We keep telling you that, and, for some reason, you seem to think that sick means having a cold or a bellyache. He's got a broke bone and I believe it's pressing through the skin. Every time we move him, you can see the pain on his face. A full bath ain't high on the list right now. Keeping him quiet and comfortable and getting broth into him's been all we can do."

The old man's eyes opened slightly. One hand lifted from the bed. When Mrs. Carpenter bent to take the hand, he waved her away and said: "I'm going to die in peace, god dammit. Now, leave me alone." He shifted his head toward Maggie. "Where's English gone to? I need him."

"You have turned my husband against me," Mrs. Carpenter accused Maggie. "This is why I want him moved. You have done everything you could to keep him here while you pampered him, and more than likely fed him drugs so that his mind is cloudy."

Maggie heard a sound at the door and she saw Burn peek into the cabin, before entering quietly.

"You listen to me," the rancher's wife hissed at Maggie, "and don't go mooning over something that's not yours, you bitch. He's mine and I want him home."

Burn slid past the rancher's wife and stood slightly in front of Maggie. His voice was remarkably calm. "You don't call Maggie any such name, ma'am. This's her home and she's been taking good care of your husband. No call for such talk."

For that he received a slap from Rose Carpenter. A trickle of blood began to come out his nose. He used his sleeve to wipe it away. "Ma'am, I believe you best leave the house. You go sit with your man, Rogelio, outside. He's got good sense, and he listens to your husband. Perhaps it's time you did the same."

It was a sight to see. All that boning and stitching and padding taking flight out the door.

The woman was so angry she hit the doorjamb with her shoulder.

Burn shook his head. Maggie laughed softly.

"Let's fix that nose bleed, and then we'll see to Mister Carpenter," Maggie said. "I want him to know she's not going to take him from here. Not when we've gone this far."

As she stopped Burn's nosebleed, she mustered the courage finally to ask him what had been on her mind. "Why'd you get in so deep, Burn? It ain't just me, I know that." If nothing else, Maggie Heber was practical.

Burn held her hand quietly. "I know Haydock Carpenter . . . know his truth . . . and he ain't afraid of death. She is. She's terrified. Hell. . . ." He stopped and looked down. "Sorry, Maggie. I'm acting as bad as her." He took a breath.

She shook her hand loose from his and wiped at a fresh trickle of blood.

"It ain't the leg killing him," Burn continued. "I think it's new times and ideas that he don't like. And marrying that woman was a wrong choice, and he knows it. She'll talk him to death if he gets taken back to their home. He's safe here . . . at home in what he knows, what he remembers from his past . . . a rough, but clean and honest place. You're a good woman who cares. He trusts that. Trusts me . . . that I'll bury him right. No fancied-up coffin or procession. A pine box and a dirt hole under a tree. She'll want the big hoopla . . . a procession and a preacher and a black hearse. Hell, she's already got the matching black horses." He used his sleeve again to wipe at his nose. It was sore, but, being so close to Maggie, the pain seemed more a pleasure.

"That doesn't answer my question," Maggie said.

Then a low voice came from the bed, and they both turned to Carpenter. "My question, too, boy. Why?"

There was no escape from the question for Burn. He sat down on the chair so hard that the back slats *creaked*.

"My whole family died when I was maybe thirteen. Same illness got me, too, but I didn't die." He laughed at the foolishness of his statement— of course, he hadn't died. He began again. "I went to work mustanging." He was aware of how much he was leaving out, but those details were only important to him. Maybe later, with her, some-time in the future. . . . He shook his head.

Maggie shifted closer to him, put her hand on his shoulder, but he shrugged it off. There was no helping him through this. "Stayed clear of folks, caught my horses, and trained 'em, sold 'em, made me a good life alone, like I wanted."

Now it was getting even tougher and he felt a tightening in his belly. The old wounds began to ache as if new. His mouth felt dried out as he realized the long confession was more for Maggie than the old man—to give her a chance to get out if she wanted.

"Got run into barbed wire . . . nearly killed me. Good folks took me in, foul temper and all, and they nursed me close to four months' time." He swallowed as saliva built up his mouth now. "Took another try at dying to teach me 'bout living, allowing folks to love me . . . to love them. I stayed to that place a long time, longer'n any other place in my whole life. Nineteen years and more." He couldn't look at Maggie. "No, I wasn't married or father to a family. Uncle, I guess, to four kids and a good friend . . . a woman I once loved."

Then his mind seemed to go empty. The Hildahls were gone, their faces barely remembered, and he'd known this woman in front of him only a few days, but they'd lived through a year's worth of learning.

Then: "There's love in this cabin. You and your children, ma'am."

The old man grunted his agreement, while Maggie seemed embarrassed, rubbing her hands together, looking at the floor.

Burn swallowed hard just as a racket came from the yard outside. Loud voices, cursing, a *clunking* explosion that sent Burn to his feet and running out the door, wishing he had a pistol rather than that broken-open, useless shotgun he'd liked to have killed the woman with.

• • •

Riding the mare was the closest thing to perfection that Ruthie had ever experienced in her young life. She loved horses, loved sharing their freedom, and, while old Roany did his best and carried her to places she could never reach on her own, Beauty . . . well, she floated and danced and Ruthie wasn't aware of being a rider so much as being part of Beauty's existence.

Ruthie would breathe and the mare would stop. She would look to the right, and Beauty would follow her eyes' direction. She'd stand at the smallest voice, wait while Ruthie made up her mind.

Mostly, though, Beauty trotted, just like she'd been told she would do by her mister. She knew the trot could cover distance and not tire horse or rider. Ruthie recognized the importance of her errand, knew that a doctor was needed to take care of Mr. Carpenter and settle the feud that seemed to be taking place in their lives. Adults were peculiar and Ruthie didn't think much of the Carpenter woman who couldn't see her husband's distress or understand it.

Even though a kid, Ruthie knew things. Like that her two brothers at home were fools. She never listened to their plans or accepted their word as truth. And she knew that her ma liked men, but Ruthie thought that this one had something different to him. None of that loafing around. Her ma looked at him like . . . well, sometimes it made Ruthie blush and she was too young to feel these things.

Mr. Carpenter wasn't hard to understand at all and it puzzled Ruthie why his ugly wife was making such a fuss. The man was purely ill. You only had to look at his hands, pale even though they'd been worked their whole life. But no color was there, only blued veins on the back, like thick worms. He was dying, she knew that. Her riding for the doctor . . . well, there was no hope. But her ma, she wouldn't give up, and Burn English, he tended to the old rancher like a son or good friend.

Ruthie heard them talking together those few times the old man was awake and alert. The subject was usually horses, and something about the mare's pappy, her sire they called it, and what a great horse he'd been. This surprised Ruthie since she was certain sure that the two men didn't know each other. But they sure liked talking horses together, the old man gasping between his words, Beauty's owner patient, letting the old man talk and remember.

The track widened out through a series of small grassy hills, taking the low and easy way through for the carriages she knew traveled this way. Soft dirt, few rocks, no hills. Ruthie had been saving up, walking Beauty until the mare's neck was no longer damp. She'd been puzzling over how to ask. On Roany, she had to use a stick or the end of the reins and kick as hard and often as possible to achieve that slow even lope that Roany had in him once in a great while.

Although no instructions had been given by English as to how to gallop Beauty, Ruthie was pretty sure that kicking the mare would get her bucked off, so she leaned forward and drew her legs against the mare's sides and whispered about how fast she wanted to go. In response Beauty gave a leap, and, if Ruthie hadn't grabbed the horn, she would have tumbled over the mare's rump as the mare shook her head and took huge strides, her whole body seeming to crouch lower to the ground.

The wind took Ruthie's breath, her eyes watered, and she didn't dare let go of the saddle or the reins to wipe them. Briefly she could hear the lightest *thump* as each hoof hit the powdered dirt, but then it was all wind and nothing in the world could catch her.

A wide turn between two hills, and then out onto plains of rolling grass with the trail heading down the middle. In the distance Ruthie could see a black shape coming at her and Beauty. It was fast and quick. But there were no horses in harness, just a black carriage traveling on its own.

Beauty seemed to have her own thoughts about the oncoming monster for she skidded to a stop as the thing got closer, and Ruthie ended up on

Beauty's neck, holding to her mane and one ear while she struggled to regain the saddle behind her. The black carriage stopped itself a good distance away, just as Ruthie found the saddle. While she rearranged herself, Beauty, unexpectedly walked forward, almost close enough to touch the steaming, rumbling machine. Ruthie could just hear the mare's snorting over her own pounding heart.

"You all right, young lady?" the man in the machine said.

Ruthie heard the words and found them an insult. "'Course, I'm all right. It's that thing you're in causing all the trouble."

The rider, or whatever he was called, must have been used to people feeling that way, for he smiled as Ruthie let herself relax in the saddle. Beauty reached out very carefully and rubbed the shiny black front of the thing with her nose, snorting, pawing once, then standing quietly at Ruthie's command.

"My name is Doctor Oliphant, miss. And you are . . . ?"

He knew his manners, this doctor.

Ruthie beat him to the question. "You going to the Heber cabin to see about old man Carpenter?"

"Why, yes, but . . . how did you know?"

"I was sent to fetch you."

He shook his head. "Young lady . . . for you have yet to introduce yourself."

She interrupted even though her ma had taught

her not to do so with adults, saying that they didn't like it. It didn't matter if you were a kid and got interrupted, though, but that was a talk she should have with her ma, and not this man.

"My name is Ruth Mary Heber . . . and that Mister Carpenter . . . he's at our house and his wife wants to take him home. We got a man staying with us. He owns this mare." Here she patted Beauty, who seemed to bow her head in receiving the attention. "He keeps telling her . . . the wife, that is . . . the old man is too sick to travel, but that mean Missus Carpenter, she keeps coming over and causing trouble." She took a deep breath. "Who told you, anyhow?"

The doctor wiped his face, and then smiled politely. "A young man from the Carpenter ranch . . . name of Arcy . . . rode to my office late last night and gave me the information. I had other patients and only now was able to make the journey to see him . . . Mister Carpenter that is."

It took a moment's thought to gather the courage to ask the question, but then she just blurted out what was on her mind. "What is that thing you're in and how does it move?"

His smile came again, making him look almost nice. "It is a horseless carriage, or automobile, and it runs by an engine underneath where your lovely mare touched her muzzle."

Ruthie patted Beauty's neck. "Ain't she something?"

Despite his riding in a machine, the doctor seemed to appreciate a good horse. "You must run a fine ranch to have a horse like her."

"Ah, I told you she belongs to this man staying at the place. She got hurt and he wouldn't leave until she was sound enough."

"From watching you run her," Dr. Oliphant commented, "I would say the wound has healed quite sufficiently."

There was a moment of silence. Only the mare's slow breathing and a funny *ticking* from the machine interrupted the sounds of the birds and the wind.

Then finally the doctor bowed his head. "I must be getting to Mister Carpenter, Ruthie. You might want to move the mare some distance while I restart the engine." With that he climbed out of the carriage and stuck a black handle into the front end and yanked on it while something inside started to *sputter*.

It was easy to move Beauty upslope to stand away from the noise as the doctor got in and moved the machine forward and up to a speed almost as fast as Beauty had been going before coming to a stop.

With a deep sigh Ruthie reined the mare back onto the trail toward home. No more of that wonderful speed, only some trotting and walking to get her there. If she brought Beauty in hot and tired, her master might give her rightful hell.

CHAPTER FIFTEEN

Burn had seen a number of the riding machines before. One had been near his old cabin once. The confounded thing had created quite the commotion when it appeared suddenly into his silent world. On the trip north he had kept running into the noisy, smelly contraptions. Now here was another one. Smoke streaming out of its nose, bouncing along on those rubber tires, and a heavy-set man sitting inside it, wearing a duster, one like outlaws often wore to hide their guns. Then the man was climbing out of the thing, carrying a black bag. That bag told Burn it was the doctor Ruthie had been sent to fetch. A doctor, over from Mancos, in a motor car. A nasty thing, but it got him here right quickly.

But where were Ruthie and Beauty?

Burn was the first to reach the doctor, who was spending too much time brushing off dust and looking at the rodeo-like scene he'd created with his entrance. Cow ponies and *vaqueros* and the team trying to scatter from each other, anywhere to get away from the monster that had come into their midst.

Burn laughed and the doctor turned.

"Sir, you have seen one of these before?" the man of medicine asked.

"Yep . . . and luckily I ain't on a horse this time." Burn paused before asking: "You seen a girl on a pretty bay mare? She all right? The girl?"

"Your daughter is fine, sir, and on her way back to your home. That mare must have also seen an automobile before, for she did not spook. She walked right up to the automobile and sniffed it. Your daughter is quite an accomplished horse-woman. I watched her come across the valley. She and that mare were flying and it was a pleasure to watch." The pleasantries being over, he said: "I'm Doctor Oliphant. Would you be so kind as to show me to the invalid."

Burn had to think on that one, but then the Carpenter woman approached and he understood. He took hold of the doctor by the arm and spun him around, directing him inside the cabin, closing the door firmly in Mrs. Carpenter's angry face.

It came to him then that the doctor had assumed Ruthie was his child. A warmth settled in him.

Maggie was there to pull back the torn curtain. Even taking a short breath, you could smell the infection. Burn opened his mouth to defend Maggie and what they'd been doing for Carpenter. But the doctor just held up his hand, settled into the chair next to the bed, and studied Carpenter.

Carpenter studied the man right back. The doctor was a youngster, not what he'd expected. When he had heard the commotion caused by his arrival, he figured either the town of Mancos had grown some recently or the doctor himself was a wealthy man. Owning one of those vehicles out here was risky, even if it made sense. Time could save a life.

The doctor nodded and lifted up Haydock's hand, holding it carefully, thumb and first finger together right where a bone had been broken years back when a steer had horned his bay gelding and brought them both down. Maybe thirty years ago. Damn, it had hurt. He still missed that horse, too. He had been gutted so bad that Haydock had had to shoot the sorry beast. Shot the steer, too, out of rage. Had steak for a week and grinned over every bite. That bay was one of the best horses he had ever raised.

The doctor's face wasn't looking very promising. Haydock tried a grin, but the doctor only shook his head.

"Mister Carpenter. . . ." It was an old voice in a young face. The man had seen too much already. "Your pulse is quite weak. I fear there has been damage to your heart over the years."

At least the young sawbones wasn't a coward. He told the truth to his patient instead of hiding it or confiding it only to the family.

"Hell, doc, I know that. Been lying here feeling that flutter. Don't matter much. I had me a good life, and getting sent out by a horse suits me just fine."

Dr. Oliphant shook his head. Such candid talk from a patient wasn't usual in his practice.

Good-looking youngster, Carpenter thought. *Late thirties . . . dark hair . . . blue eyes, sturdy but not fat, not like most o' the men who ride in them vehicles, instead of working for their living.* Haydock had a feeling the doctor was doing the same thing he was—looking him over, checking out the scars and wrinkles, and making his own judgment.

"Let me look at the leg, Mister Carpenter," the doctor said, and turned his head to address Maggie. "Ma'am, would you boil me some water on the stove and bring fresh linens?"

Where else did he think she'd boil water? Maggie wondered. But it was a request being made by an educated man, even if it didn't seem that getting an education made sense to her. Surely the man could see there was a cook stove with a kettle on it, shoved to the back. But Maggie was quick to do the chore, not wanting anything to make Mr. Carpenter suffer more than he had to.

Thoughts were circling, making Haydock dizzy. He flinched when the doctor cut open the bindings over the wood splints Mrs. Heber and English had used. The doctor's quick intake of breath, plus the stench told Haydock what he already knew. He tried to push his upper body up off the bed, but the doctor placed a small, almost feminine hand on his chest and Haydock couldn't push against it.

"Mister Carpenter, there's no need to tell you, but I will in any case. These people did exactly the right thing. Only . . . it's a shame I was not sent for immediately. The man sent last night by your wife said the accident occurred three days ago. Is that right?"

Haydock nodded, even though he had no idea how long he'd been with the Hebers. It was all he could do. The weight of the hand still pushed against his lungs making breathing difficult.

"Ma'am. . . ." Dr. Oliphant removed his hand to twist about in the chair to speak to Maggie Heber.

Haydock lay back on the bed, thankful for the pillow under his head, holding him up.

"Ma'am . . . this's a good job of splinting. The water . . . ?"

Minutes later, Haydock was feeling good. The air was soothing to the stinking wound, as was the warm water the doctor used to bathe it. Those feminine hands were softer than the callused hands of English, the blunt hands of the woman. His eyes grew heavy as the doctor wiped his face with a strange-smelling ointment. And finally the pain of the broken bone didn't matter.

"Did you move him around much?" Oliphant asked of Maggie and Burn.

"No," Burn said. "We kept him to the bed once we got him inside. I was the one tended mostly to his needs . . . you know, nature calling . . . and I fed him. We tried to keep him still, but there were a couple a times we had a dust-up in the yard and I'd find him trying to sit up. Guess maybe he heard familiar voices."

"Sometime after you put on the splint . . . excellent job by the way . . . the bone finally pushed its way through the flesh. Couldn't be helped, especially if he moved the leg."

Burn heard the judgment behind the studied praise. He thought of Rose Carpenter's rough treatment on her first visit. He took his frustration out on the doctor. "Mister, we ain't idiots. We knew what we was doing wouldn't be the best of doctoring, but it was all we could do. Don't go trying to act high and mighty 'cause of your learning. If I'd had the sense, I would have opened up that binding, checked everything was all right. Too much going on. So don't sugarcoat what you're saying. He's infected. Hell of a mess. But if the old man's heart were all right, he'd make it through." Here Burn paused, before continuing. "His heart ain't good. I can see it in his breathing, in the color in his face. No matter what we done . . . right or wrong . . . nothing can fix the heart."

Such observations from a rough cowhand were highly unusual, and under the current circumstances Thompson Oliphant, graduate of the prestigious Harvard Medical School and fresh from a practice in Boston, was quite impressed with the man's powers of observation. Whoever or whatever this man was, his life had been of the mind as much as the obvious hard work that had physically taken its toll on him.

Burn felt sheepish now, but had to ask: "How long's he got, Doc?"

It went against all learned medical practice to speak of such details in front of the patient, but he heard a grunt from the bed, and, when he turned to look at Carpenter, he saw a small nod. Then a voice gave consent.

"You tell 'em, Doc. I 'ready know." Carpenter started coughing, before he could continue. Then: "He knows, too. It's that woman outside . . . my wife, you're gonna have trouble convincing."

Dr. Oliphant nodded, and lightly touched the back of the old man's hand.

"You tell us . . . ," Burn said, "then you go out and fight that there dragon. She's been giving her husband fits because she wants to take him home. And she's been cursing Maggie somethin' terrible in her own home . . . in front of her child. I mean Ruthie, the girl who went looking for you." Before Dr. Oliphant could get his thoughts together, the cowboy continued. "Tell her maybe he'll be better in a couple of days. We know the end is going to be soon . . . maybe that way she'll go home and not bother him no more."

An ethical dilemma. One the doctor had never

faced before. He looked at the patient, whose bluish eyes were blinking open and closed. Then there was a smile from the man. "Got him a plan, by God," Carpenter said. "And it's a good 'un."

Dr. Oliphant rose carefully from the chair, after having discarded the splint and rebinding the broken limb with fresh medical bandages. The wound was clean, packed with medication so it should not be uncomfortable for the next few hours. "Ma'am." He bowed to Maggie who had remained silent throughout the examination. Abruptly he turned to the small man who seemed to know exactly what the patient wanted. He took his time, studying this odd specimen, staring deeply into his face, seeing compassion, practicality, a sense of humor. And something beyond that when the woman moved close to him. He was dark, well-muscled for such a small man, with quite outsize hands. It was those hands that demanded the doctor's attention, and curiosity overrode manners and decency. Dr. Oliphant reached for one of Burn's scarred hands and oddly enough the man was co-operative. The doctor ran his fingers along the scars, turned the hand over, and pushed back the sleeve. The double ridges disappeared up the forearm.

"This was bad. How long ago?"

"Nineteen years."

"Any more such scars?"

"Yeah, but I ain't showing them to you. They're

here . . . and here." The left hand swept across his belly, and then down his thigh with an upward swing across his buttocks.

Oliphant shuddered. "Nineteen years."

"Yeah."

A lot was left unsaid. The doctor turned Burn's wrist over, holding the hand a moment longer, finding it difficult to imagine that someone could survive such violence and brutality.

"How?"

"Ran a horse straight into that bob wire." A pause. "Killed the horse . . . should 'a' killed me."

"What medicines were used?"

"Mostly flour . . . to stop the bleeding." He stopped, as if something was remembered. "Then warm bathing. A lot of prayers from some good people . . . purple coneflower from a *curandera*."

"Unorthodox, but obviously effective." Oliphant let go of Burn's hand.

Burn only shook his head. "Long time in the past."

The doctor headed out of the cabin, got to the door, and turned. "That's how you knew?"

"Yeah."

To his surprise, the doctor found it was snowing, very lightly, the softest of flakes. He stood a moment and turned his face up to the sky, delighting at the points of cold caressing his face.

There was a well-endowed woman sitting in the front seat of a wagon. The bed of the wagon was

234

padded with straw and blankets. It looked as though a horse had attempted to make a meal of it. He steeled himself and walked to the wagon.

Her arms folded over her considerable bosom, her eyes straight ahead, Mrs. Carpenter barely glanced at him. She didn't give him a chance to take more than a few steps. "I want my husband home with me this minute," she announced. "The charade has gone on long enough. Those two do not have the right to keep me from tending to my own man."

She was a force of Nature. Thompson Oliphant inhaled, let out a small gust of air, and then rubbed his hands together. He put on his best medical face and, in no uncertain terms, said: "Ma'am, I can understand your concern and your wish to transport your husband to his familiar surroundings." He had a feeling the woman had made what must have been a useable bachelor home into a fanciful showplace of horsehair sofas and carved chairs and no place comfortable for a man to sit. He smiled briefly, not wishing to appear ghoulish. "It appears, ma'am, your husband is resting comfortably, and, perhaps if you and these men would return in the late morning tomorrow, you can visit. And in a few more days . . . who knows. But you really can't move him today." *There,* he thought, *not a lie in anything I've told her.* She would read whatever reality she wanted in the words.

A man of Spanish descent approached. He gave a polite if brief bow, to which Oliphant responded with a tip of his bowler.

"*Señor*, are you saying that our *señor*, he will recover?"

Ah, Oliphant thought to himself, *another man who thinks*. This would be difficult if he was to maintain his no-lies doctrine.

"Sir?"

"Ah, *sí* . . . my name is Rogelio Vigil."

"Doctor Thompson Oliphant."

They exchanged a handshake.

The doctor cleared his throat before beginning. "Mister Carpenter's broken bone, unfortunately, has pushed itself through the skin and become infected. I have cleaned and packed the infection and do not expect it to cause him any more discomfort." *There,* he thought, *that's direct and true even if not responsive to his question.* He could see in Rogelio's eyes disbelief. He thought it best to continue speaking to keep the man from asking any more questions, which would result in having to lie. "Sir, Mister Carpenter is resting well, in no pain for the time being. A good night's sleep is what he needs." Enough, no more, or lies would begin to spill out from his mouth.

Rogelio shook his head and turned, looking at the seated woman, who tried to appear as if she were disinterested in the conversation. It was Rogelio who made the decision. He walked to the wagon and climbed onto the seat, picking up the lines.

"Until tomorrow, *señor*," he said, and glanced at Mrs. Carpenter.

The crew of riders and their skittish horses fell into a loose formation around the back of the wagon. Several of the horses bucked, but the riders sat their mounts easily. The doctor drove a car because he had never mastered this particular art of horsemanship. So he admired the men's skills, but without any sense of envy.

Jonas kicked his brother. They had settled themselves inside the barn where they could watch and listen. They knew it wasn't their fight, but still. . . .

"We should o' taken a swing at a couple of them . . . *vaqueros* they call themselves," Jonas said. "Don't like them riding in here like they're better'n us."

Tad had a different point of view. "Them's right nice stock they was riding. If we got ourselves work riding for a good brand, hell, Jonas, we could be riding bronc's just like them."

Jonas grumbled: "Still think we needed to beat on some o' them fellas."

Tad shoved his brother, pushing him off the half barrel they were using as a seat. "Jonas, don't be stupid. They didn't do nothing to us. Ain't no cause to pound on 'em."

Jonas shoved back at his brother. "I like that

machine the doc's driving. I snuck a look till the horses got calmed. Me, I don't want to ride no horse. That machine looks to be a real good way to travel."

Tad reached down and grabbed Jonas's arm, pulling him back and sprawling him across the barrel seat. Jonas immediately pulled back and tightened his fists, figuring on a brawl with his older brother.

Tad leaned away from him. "I ain't fighting . . . just figuring. We got nothing here. Ma's strong on that new man, and, though I don't take much to him, he's kind to Ruthie."

There wasn't much more that needed saying. The two brothers might fight each other with intent to hurt, but, as close as they were, words didn't need to be spoken.A few minutes later, Jonas stood. "Time to get moving, Tad. We'll tell Ma . . . or wait for Ruthie to get back and tell her, and then she can tell Ma."

Tad looked up at his brother and said: "She's got English and old Carpenter. We don't need to give her more worry. I'll go tell her. You figure out what gear we can take."

Maggie's eyes teared up as she drew Tad close to her. He could smell her tears, her sadness. Smelled something like the medicine they had put on that old man. Tad was embarrassed by being so close. She was so female it hurt right through him. Old enough to know what all that flesh was for, and angry at himself for thinking about that and his ma at the same time.

"I know, Tad. It's time. You and Jonas . . . well, it's time. Jonas likes automobiles. I saw him walking 'round the doc's."

Looking past his shoulder, Tad saw English staring at his ma before he slid behind the curtain where the old man lay. Tad heard the scrape of the wood chair and then the old man's weak voice. Nice of the man to step away from a boy saying good bye to his ma. *Might be this one will stay,* Tad thought.

Maggie helped Tad bundle up their few clothes and put together a bag of foodstuffs to keep them going for a while. She let him take the rifle, but told him to leave the shotgun, because it wasn't any good for hunting game. They both laughed, then her eyes teared up again. He couldn't stand it, so he lurched in to kiss her cheek, and missed, getting her ear, but it was all he could bear. Then he ran, hauling the burlap bags over his shoulder.

When he heard Maggie crying, Burn held his breath. He half stood until the old man's hand grabbed him and pulled him down, saying: "Let her cry . . . be alone. Time. Then go find her."

Burn listened to her footsteps, the lightness of sound, her particular step, her way of moving. He could imagine her going through the cabin door, standing a moment, staring at the empty yard. If the boys were already gone, she would follow the path they had taken with her wet gaze, study the settling dust, knowing her children had walked that very spot as they left her.

He turned back and stared into the glazed eyes. "You need anything?" Burn kept his voice low, not wanting Maggie to hear him and think she was needed inside. He and the old man, they could take care of almost anything.

It was Ruthie who found her mother crying, huddled in a corner of the barn, nesting in the sweet hay with a white towel on her face. Ruthie was scared at first, for she was standing right next to her ma and she didn't even seem to know that she was there. She was sobbing so hard that it sounded to Ruthie like her ma's heart was broken. Immediately she decided to go kick that English cowboy, give him hell for hurting Ma. Yet it was easy to see that her ma was taken by him, although other than the way he rode a horse, Ruthie didn't see anything special to the man. Just another one hanging around, except that he had a great horse that he might let her ride again, and he worked for his keep.

She sneezed which startled her ma. Maggie pulled the towel away from her wet face and cried out: "Oh, Ruthie!" At this, Ruthie sat down next to her ma and hugged her.

"Tad and Jonas," Maggie began, "they left just

now before you got back . . . took their clothes and some food and headed out . . . going the same way that doc rode that machine. Tad told me Jonas was dead set on learning how to ride one of those things."

Ruthie snuggled in closer to her ma, sighing and thinking: *It's about time.* Then she said: "I saw them and I said good bye and good luck. But, Mama . . . I think you drive that beast . . . it ain't alive enough to ride."

Maggie rubbed her hands through Ruthie's hair, catching her fingers in all the tangles. "Not been paying you enough attention, have I? All this . . . fuss . . . it took me away from what's important."

Although she knew the answer, Ruthie asked anyway. "He going to stay with us?"

Her ma's response surprised her. "I don't know, Ruthie. He hasn't asked or said nothing." Then she said what Ruthie wanted to hear. "I hope so."

Good, Ruthie thought, *he stays, I get to ride that mare.*

CHAPTER SIXTEEN

Burn stayed in the chair, letting Carpenter's gnarled hand remain on his arm. There was still life inside those bones and ligaments, a deep breath occasionally, the thin chest rising, falling.

It was getting dark outside, and Maggie had built up a good fire, told the girl to feed out extra hay to the roan and the mare, it was going to be cold tonight. She asked Burn if he wanted supper. He shook his head, but in a few minutes Ruthie brought him a cup filled with a thick soup, anyway. He could identify chunks of soft squash, something green, bits and pieces of the game birds. It tasted good, so he offered the old man a spoonful of broth.

"No point now. It's done," Haydock Carpenter said.

Burn got up once, about midnight. He had to, and the old man smiled, understanding. Maggie took the chair while Burn went to the outhouse. It was damned cold out there, and, coming back in, he appreciated the cabin's tight warmth.

Maybe it was an hour later, maybe three, but he awoke quickly to a twitch from the fingers that were clasped tightly on his wrist. Then the grasp loosened. Harsh breathing gone, eyes motionless, empty. No one else was there to witness. Maggie had wrapped herself in blankets near the fire where the boys usually slept. Ruthie was dreaming up in her loft.

Burn carefully arranged Carpenter's hands across his chest, shut his eyes, drew up the light quilt to cover the gaunt face. He faced going to the barn to his own nest of blankets and the horses' poor shared warmth, the thin winds that found every crack in the wood framing and crawled into bed with him. But, instead, he took one thick quilt, laying on a chair near the fire, and used a seat cushion as a pillow to make his own pallet. He set a few small logs on the fire, not enough to throw sparks, but enough to keep the coals burning, building life-giving heat.

It was sunrise. The air in the cabin was chilled. There was no sound but a rustle. Then a nudge against his back. Burn remained still, waiting. A soft voice tickled his ear. "I can keep us warm. You want into my bed now?"

He took a long time answering. "What about Ruthie . . . ?"

"Child knows, don't mind. She said yesterday she hopes you'll stay on."

"He died not long ago."

"I know. Heard you stepping around. Figured as much." She pressed up against him, her loose breasts heavy, warming two spots on his back. "You all right, Burn? It ain't easy sitting with death, but he wanted you with him. You two knew each other." She stopped talking, pressed closer. "I sat with my first husband. . . ." Her voice died out and her body shivered and the effect on Burn wasn't one of grief. He rolled over to face her with all the intention of talk, but she simply kissed him and it was too much.

Burn pulled free from the embrace, feeling eerily like he was looking down on his actions, as if he was watching the two of them from above, noting their positions, curious as to why a man was resisting such a woman. He wasn't a prude. He didn't think he was. But this was too much.

"Burn, I got *five* sons, all growed and gone now. And a daughter who means more to me than my own life. But I'm also alive, and a man was meant to have a good woman. You're telling me by pulling away, I ain't a good woman . . . least not good enough for you?"

She amazed him. Her tone wasn't bitter, not hurt, not sad. Just facts—clear as any woman could speak to a man. He owed her an honest response.

So he rolled away from her, conscious of his body's arousal, embarrassed by his flesh even as he fought to keep from touching her. "I ain't much to look at, Maggie. Me, not my face so much as my body . . . what you see and feel when . . . well. . . ."

"You told the doc while I was standing there. I can imagine."

"No, you can't. I have to force my own self to look at the scarring. No woman wants a man cut up the way I am."

She pulled back so she could see his face better in the fire light.

"You trying to tell me something's been cut off?" she asked. "Don't seem that way to me."

As a log flamed up, he could see she was smiling as she spoke, and Burn hoped she couldn't see his face redden.

"Everything's where it needs to be, but I was cut up something terrible. Makes me want to vomit when I have to touch the scars. Been almost twenty years and I still can't deal with them, and I can't ask you or anyone to take me this way."

She was stubborn. "Now that doc," Maggie pressed, "he grabbed onto the scarred hand and arm and wanted to see more. It didn't bother him none at all."

Burn tried to look away from her, but she put one hand on the side of his face and held him steady while she talked. "It weren't that he was a doc. . . . It's that you're a good man, nothing more. He saw it for all his fancy airs . . . and my daughter knows. Even your mare, she knows." She put her hand over her mouth, then grinned and that gesture pleased Burn. Something came to her then. Her face went still, her eyes looked sad. "You telling me it's been that long since you've been with a woman?"

A question no one had ever asked. A subject he'd never shared. Her face was close to his and he could feel her breathing. Her eyes were closed now, as if willing him to talk and giving him room.

"No." He took a big gulp. His face was flushed, his hands sweating. "Whores don't care. It's money to them . . . nothing more. Flesh means dollars. They never noticed the scars. Don't know if they even saw them."

She rested her hand on his mouth. "Enough. I don't want to hear this."

It was a struggle for him. "You asked."

"Yes, and I needed to know, but it's too sad. A good man like you. So alone."

He moved to hold her, and she rested her head on his chest. His body calmed, his skin eased, the flush disappeared. She didn't care.

"Let me see your belly," she said a few minutes later. "Just what's under the shirt. Ruthie told me what you looked like. Imagine, my own daughter spying on a naked man." She shook her head, barely able to keep from laughing. " 'Course, we all figured you was kinda crazy for swimming in that pond this time a year." She was laughing now as her fingers slowly unbuttoned his shirt, then the top of the long johns he wore. True to her word she did not push below the waist of his jeans, unbuttoned so he could sleep in some comfort. She rolled him onto his back and pushed the covers away so he lay exposed.

A small chill brushed across the hairs on his chest. He shivered. His fists tightened, and his throat was so dry he couldn't swallow. She kissed his mouth, then his neck. She said nothing, only kissed him again on his chest, let her fingers touch the side of his mouth, then stroke his jaw, his cheek, until he felt his own tears torn free and he wanted to wipe them away, but she used the lightest touch to do it for him. No one had ever touched him with such gentleness, such intimacy. Not even when he'd been injured.

"Burn, I want to give this to you. To a good man who will be constant." She sighed, tucked her head near his chin, spoke into his naked chest. "I'm faithful to my man, I just ain't shown good sense up till now."

They both fell asleep.

Burn woke, wrapped in the quilt, with her hand against his belly, right on the deepest scarring. He slid free of her, rolling himself out of the quilt. He looked at Maggie and saw her lick her lips as she slept. Worn out by the past few days, he figured. He didn't blame her.

He left the house, bootless, cursing the cold ground till he found a place to sit, pull on his boots, and shuck into his coat. At least the light dusting of snow had melted. He didn't mind that he'd have to leave behind a few things that were still in the house. He needed thinking time, a clear head, his body not wanting her so badly it made it impossible to think. Those kisses on his exposed past, her gentle acceptance challenged his knowledge of himself.

Beauty was still chewing on wisps of last night's hay so he felt no conscience in saddling her without a morning feed. He tied on the few items he could find. Hell and damn, he had to get out, find a place to think.

The ugly Appaloosa gelding nickered sadly when Burn led Beauty from the barn. Burn was grinning despite himself, running his hands over the mare before he saddled up. He found no swelling, no heat in the hard legs, no ill effects from yesterday's gallop. He was careful to check the edge of pink skin still remaining from the wire cut. There was no flinching when he tightened his hand around the bone. The mare leaned down and lipped the top of his head where his black hair was too long, flying loose, in need of a good shearing.

If he stayed, Maggie would offer to cut his hair, like she had done with the boys. Burn couldn't imagine bearing even that small intimacy without the need for more. He barely had the willpower to leave.

He wasn't much and had no illusions about what he could give her. When she woke up, he didn't want to be there to have her see him in full daylight. He didn't want to see what would cross her face—relief, disgust, a certain distance? It was time he was gone. Those had been pity kisses. They had to have come from her sudden loneliness, her recent losses. He couldn't fill the holes in her life. Sitting with that old man had taken all he had had.

He was bent on heading north, knowing full well a big storm with drifts and a howling wind would freeze him solid. His fingers raked the mare's coat, noting the long winter hairs under which the skin was warm and dry. She'd do fine. It would be Burn himself who would come to grief. Deep inside was a knowledge of choosing death. He'd been its witness last night. It was close, waiting on his decision.

The mare wanted to buck when he stepped into the saddle. Burn grinned, let out a bit of rein, and Beauty crow-hopped across the yard. Without looking back, he waved his arm, and pushed the mare into a run. They were gone in a hurry, pounding up dust.

The mare was sensible enough to come to her easy jog. Burn patted her warmed neck, smelled the thick taste of salt through the winter hair. No more galloping for them. She'd be chilled come evening and he'd have to hand walk her and rub her down. It would be damned stupid to mistreat a good horse in such a manner.

A few trees, long yellowed grasses, a narrow game trail where Beauty let each hoof fall in her easy rhythm, taking them both some place else, some place where no one would get into Burn's heart.

The mare stuttered to a halt. Burn got thrown

forward, then back. The mare shook violently as if he'd startled her. He apologized by stroking her neck and she shook again until he was loose in the saddle. She had stopped in Salt Valley where only a short time ago he'd found a private heaven. But it had been interrupted, destroyed, complicated by humans and their idiocy. He wanted to rein the mare around and gallop up the slanted ridge and across the edge of the valley where the old man's house sat watching, empty now, even with the unknowing widow living there.

He thought about Maggie's cabin nestled against the north winds, protected by the long-running ridge, facing south for warmth, shaded by the open-weave ramada in the summer. Soft winds that blew out the human scent, doors to be closed tight, a fireplace that drew well enough for good heat, special stews, pies made with fresh apples or cherries picked and dried, sweetened with town molasses.

The mare shook again. Burn climbed down, feeling every tired bone, every old break or wound. He walked toward the familiar cotton-wood, leafless now, a cloak of dried leaves rustling, some lifting and then falling back as he had stepped across them to reach the tree's comfort. Then he sat, his back against the trunk of the tree.

Beauty grazed, stepping carefully around the

trailing reins. Burn watched her, knowing he needed to get up and go to her, remove the bridle and hang it on the horn, put on her hobbles so she wouldn't take a notion to bolt again and get caught in wire, or return to the cabin and the old Appaloosa and the familiar home corral.

He sat and studied the mare. So much like her papa. A lean neck tied into a good shoulder, defined withers smoothing into a short back. The hindquarters were different than her sire's had been, higher up at the groin, leaner through the stifle like most mares. He figured it was to give room for growing a baby. Like a woman was narrow in the waist, wide in the hip, to support life. He pushed his mind back into judging the mare. Nice gaskin tied into a clean hock. Strong bones and good hoofs. He wished he could breed her to a racing stallion. It would be a good start for another herd.

Burn eased himself lower against the cotton-wood trunk, finding just the right spot where his spine fitted into old grooves. He leaned his head back, letting his hat push forward and then slide down to rest between his legs. He needed to move on, ride north, keep Beauty at an even trot, jog a few miles, then walk again, not letting her get sweaty while putting miles between himself and the cabin, the girl child . . . Maggie.

There wasn't long before he turned restless. His back itched. His butt was cold from the freezing ground. Haydock Carpenter was dead, lying behind a tattered curtain. Maggie would have to clean the flesh and see again what the loss of life meant to a man. Nothing there.

Wasn't that much left for Burn now. A year maybe, or a month, even just days, depending on the northern storms, his own despair, the mare's recovered energy. Hiding behind the scattered thoughts was the knowledge that he'd left Maggie with Haydock Carpenter's lifeless body.

Beauty lifted her head and whinnied, her ears pricked, winter grass hanging from her mouth. Burn sat up. It was time, she was telling him. He stood. Then, hearing that particular sound, he turned and looked up at the ridge. An ugly Appaloosa head appeared, long skull and loose ears, those damned blue eyes. The Appaloosa stepped into his ugly lope when he saw the mare.

Maggie was bouncing with the roan's gait, grabbing mane, white legs showing above gray lisle stockings, thighs gripping the mottled hide. She had the horse steered toward Burn, but, when she saw him waiting, she smiled at him and her concentration was lost and she came off, landing in the matted grasses, laughing even as Burn went to her.

He rolled down beside her, barely touching her leg and shoulder as she twisted around until her face was above his and again she was smiling. He strained upward and caught at her mouth, kissed

252

her until falling back brought her down on top of him and they both were laughing.

Her mouth fitted perfectly over his, and then she spoke the words right into his mouth. "Yes, Burn English, I will marry you."

The next days were focused on getting Carpenter's body to the grieving widow and then, after that task was completed, watching her performance as they lowered the fancy coffin into the ground. Burn learned from the *vaquero*, Rogelio, that as soon as Mrs. Carpenter got back home after her first visit to the cabin, she had ordered the finest coffin she could find in Denver. She was having it delivered and had cleared out a spare bedroom to make space for it.

Most of the Rafter JX hands were going to quit the Widow Carpenter, staying on only to attend the old man's services. Then they would be gone, mounted on their private horses, beholden to no widow who had bought a coffin before her husband had up and died.

Burn knew it wasn't what the old man wanted, not this fuss and money thrown into the ground after a bunch of old bones that were going to rot and roll back into the land. But it was the widow's choice, and, this time, no one was going to tell her different.

At the funeral Maggie stood next to Burn as dirt and rocks were thrown on the ornate golden box by the *vaqueros*. She squeezed Burn's arm, looked sideways at him, and saw signs of tearing, which she would never mention to him. She recalled how he'd sat by the old man's bed, wiped his bottom, held his hand, spoon-fed him like a baby. There had never been any sense of either one being better than the other.

Standing there, Burn regretted not having been a grown man when he lost his father. Regretted having missed all of those long years together, working alongside his pa. Regretted having had the fever himself and not having been there to watch as his father had died, to have held his hand, too, at the end.

Maggie had taken Burn to her bed the day she brought him back from Salt Valley. She told Ruthie they would be marrying in a while, but for now Burn was sleeping with her ma and that was how it would be.

Ruthie grinned up at Burn and said she had figured on that when he had first come to the cabin. Took him long enough, she said. At those words, Maggie took a swipe at her child, who skipped back and said she was going to the pens to brush *her* mare.

Ruthie barely glanced at Burn. He, too, was grinning. Since the girl had ridden Beauty, there had been no way to separate them. He was looking to buy himself a new horse, and maybe find a good stallion to put to the mare. If Ruthie agreed with the idea.

Maybe Haydock's widow would need to sell a few of her horses when she realized what losing just about the whole crew meant. The old man had a papered stallion, a thoroughbred with a fine pedigree. Might be a good enough match for Beauty, Burn reasoned.

It took Burn two weeks to realize that Maggie had never mentioned marrying again. They'd slipped into a routine of hard work, building better corrals, butchering out the bull calf, and readying for winter. The boys were gone, so it fell to Burn, and sometimes Ruthie, to do the hard work.

One thing that worried him was firewood. The boys had cut down trees, but had left them lying there, rotting on the ground. That made for punky wood, but still it was better than nothing. The first week he saddled up Ruthie's old roan, with her permission, and rode out to the trees with a saw stuck in the rifle scabbard. He felt naked, but he needed the saw, and hoped he wouldn't need the rifle.

He cut the downed trees in chunks, letting the roan graze and put back on some of the weight he had lost, before winter arrived. Much as he disliked the idea, he figured on maybe doing some chores for the Carpenter woman which would help pay for extra feed over the bad months. Grass, here, turned brown and dried up in the cold.

With Ruthie's help, Burn pounded together a sledge of sorts on which he could put the wood chunks and let the roan pull them home. Once they got all the downed trees back to the cabin, he split the wood and Ruthie would stack.

One night in bed, with Maggie up close to him and her hands wandering under the covers, she sat up, surprising him. "Burn," she said, "I ain't never had a man work so hard. We got to feed you better or you're going to up and disappear." He rested his hand on her warm belly as she continued. "Now that I got you here, you ain't escaping. If I make a stew, I want you eating two bowls . . . hear me?"

It took him another week or so, but finally he decided to ask her pointblank if she ever intended to marry him. After all, she'd done the asking, sort of. He asked over that second bowl of stew. "You still planning on getting married?" She looked at him blankly, as he took a big spoon of stew and held it in mid-air. "Thought maybe this week-end, you'd have a mind to marry up with me." He swallowed and dropped the spoon back into the bowl. When he looked at her, she was smiling. He rose, leaned over the table, and kissed her. Tasted of stew and felt like a smile. He persisted. "This Saturday's a good day. You know a preacher?" She looked down, sort of away from him, and sighed, rubbing her hands together. "I thought you might let Ruthie take Beauty and go into Mancos . . . ask the preacher there. That is, if it's all right with you, and if Ruthie wants to make the ride."

They both laughed. It was set. Saturday was five days away. Burn wasn't sure he could wait.

CHAPTER SEVENTEEN

Ruthie came back in the early evening with a fool grin on her face, saying the parson would arrive early in the morning on Saturday and would be wanting breakfast before he spoke the words over the wedding pair. Maggie brushed the top of her child's head and said to run along, and that tomorrow she would have to get herself bathed. They were all taking baths tomorrow night, even if it was Friday.

Ruthie had run across her brothers in Mancos. Jonas had found what he wanted, was working with automobiles, taking bits and pieces off what made them run without horses and putting them back together. Ruthie had stayed to watch him, confused and fascinated at the same time. Grinning through a mask of grease and soot, the boss had told her that her brother was some kind of genius with the pieces of iron formed into strange shapes. Jonas had grinned up at his sister, his face and hands just as filthy as those of his boss, and said to go find Tad. He was down at the livery, Jonas thought. He'd gotten a job there.

And, yes, they were coming in for the marrying, along with the parson.

Ruthie had found Tad sweeping out a filthy aisle packed with damped hay. A harsh stench came from a half-empty line of straight-sided horse stalls. He didn't have that same light in his eyes that Jonas had and wasn't likely, he said, to give up sweeping to come home and watch Ma marry another man. Ruthie reminded her brother that this time it was a good man and a real marriage.

Tad had grunted and said that, if the damned livery boss gave him the time, he'd come. Ruthie told him Jonas's plans to travel in the buggy with the parson. She picked at her brother long enough so that he said he would do the same, God dammit.

Ruthie had stared at him, then laughed. Her brother's face got red. He knew better than to swear in front of her. Ma would have a fit, if Ruthie told.

Burn told Maggie he wanted to go down to the pond in Salt Valley and take his pre-wedding bath there. She could come with him, or stay here and take a warm bath. But it all had begun there at the pond and he wanted to stand in those waters. Felt like he needed to, he said, kind of like a ritual to make himself good enough for her.

She looked at him strangely. He tried to tell her he wasn't crazy but she said it didn't matter, if this was important, then he best go freeze his scrawny behind in the cold water, for in two days' time there would be sparks and fires enough to toast both of them.

Despite her two-day journey under Ruthie's guidance, Beauty was eager to move out after Burn saddled her. She took him straight to the pond, the same way she'd headed when he had tried to run away from Maggie and the girl. Beauty seemed to sense Burn's fear.

He didn't bother to hobble her, but stripped off the gear and watched her graze. She was comfortable here. She knew this place well. She tore into the browned grasses as if she were starving. To his experienced eye, even with all the traveling, the mare looked good, nice weight on her going into the winter. Maybe she even had had a little too much of the barn hay, for she was getting a belly, but she looked fit and ready to go.

Burn smiled to himself. Now that he had a good traveling horse, he was planning to settle down. Wasn't that the way a man's life went? He looked around, feeling a need to tell Maggie what he was thinking. She'd like the foolishness. She'd see the peculiar sadness as well as the joy of a drifter finding one place to settle.

He put his back up to the cottonwood trunk, in that fold that fitted him just right. He laid his head against the rough bark and tried to sort out his feelings.

There was nothing to him that a good woman would want. He was no better now than he had been all those years ago when Katherine had made the sensible choice. Maggie wasn't like Katherine, though. She was more direct, less afraid, which made him wonder. He shook his head, hit it against the tree trunk, and that made him laugh, which brought a whinny from Beauty. Burn himself sure wasn't any beauty, but he worked hard and they were good together in bed. That had surprised him. Women had always been terrifying to him, and those he'd known mostly were store-bought, a fact he had tried to explain to Maggie but she had put a hand over his mouth.

"I ain't asking," she had said. "And I ain't telling you 'bout my husbands. It's a natural fact, Burn English, that men and women do this. How else can there be so many of us? Don't go looking at some old woman bent double with age and forget that she had herself a lover or a husband when she was young. That shocks you? Well, tell me how men can have all the women they want and still expect us to be pure and unsoiled for them. Don't make sense at all."

There it was. Her courage and sense rolled together. He was no match for whatever Maggie Heber decided to want. And she wanted him. That was more than reason enough to marry her.

Finally it was pitch dark and the stars glittered as the winds died down and Burn was freezing, but he'd told Maggie he would bathe here in the pond, so he better, by God, do what he said he would.

It felt like his feet were freezing solid to the sand under the water with his first step in, but no one could call him a coward, so he ran in yelling, then plunged down into the cold, and came up gasping and yelling louder. Paddling and ducking under, he made a small circle of the pond and finally thought he'd suffered enough, had washed off enough of the dirt from the past few weeks. He came out of the water, pushed back his hair, wondering if she would give him a haircut or even if there was time.

Again that question. Why would she want him, a has-been *mesteñero*, broken up and scrawny, no skills that the world needed.

Then he saw the image of her face, clear as if she'd been standing in front of him, and the night wind carried her scent. He could feel her hands on him and that was reason enough to offer her his life.

• • •

She was awake, waiting for him. Their bed had new sheets and a fancy quilt, which she shyly told him she'd been working on every time he was out cutting the winter's wood. It was easy to slip in between the sheets, his body still chilled from the cleansing. The heat from her, the tender kissing, warmed him, helped him know this was right between them.

But, she told him, they could hold each other, even if that was all. After the service, with its parson and witnesses, well, they needed to be pure until then.

He would have laughed, remembering all of what they'd done together, but those pictures made his face and body heat up until he thought he understood her reserve. It wasn't right now, not when it would be legal Saturday.

On Saturday, Maggie rose early to prepare the breakfast Ruthie had promised to the parson. The last several days had been much warmer and the sun promised another unseasonably warm day. First thing, though, she wanted Burn up and out of her bed, in the barn doing chores when the parson appeared. Burn agreed to go along with her play-acting.

It wasn't long before a horse and wagon arrived, the driver in a dusty black suit. Maggie's two boys were in the back of the buggy, a two-seater befitting the parson's community position.

Ruthie was there to hold the horse, not trusting the good sense lacking in her brothers, as the man climbed out, heavy-footed and graceless, but he managed. Burn stayed at the barn where he could watch and listen even if he could not make out any distinct words. Still it seemed Ruthie was offering to see to his horse, and the man was agreeing with much head-bobbing and a wide smile. Burn already didn't like the man.

The boys shied away from their sister, wouldn't even go to the house to see their ma all prettied up to receive another man. They headed to the barn, walking some distance from each other, aware in the short time they'd been gone that this was no longer their home.

The barn was dark and smelled good. It was clean, feeling kind of like a place where they wanted to be. Jonas was the first to see English seated on an upturned barrel. He grabbed his brother's arm, tried to yank Tad around so they could escape, but the horse trainer spoke directly to them.

"Jonas, Tad. It's man-to-man time. Here it is. I'm marrying your ma. For some reason she loves me."

Then English stopped, wiped his mouth, and it occurred to Jonas that the mustanger, who had so scared him earlier with his hard edge of action and knowing, was terrified. The thought made Jonas feel more grownup and oddly inclined to sympathy.

Tad wasn't so generous. "What if I told you we don't want Ma with you. Ain't right . . . hell, she's even taller'n you. Don't suit us at all, Mister English."

Jonas shook his head, watched English closely, knowing that his decision would rest on what the man said to his older brother.

English wiped his mouth again. "You're protecting your ma, and I value that. Family is what keeps us safe, and you boys will always be her family."

At these words, Tad kind of relaxed, as if he'd been given something.

English wasn't done, though, and his next words, they shocked Jonas, must have spiked into Tad, also.

"A woman like your ma, she's a true beauty, in her heart as her flesh. She ain't meant to be alone just because her boys want her undivided among them. She's got more life to live, and I'm the one she chose. You boys, you still need to learn, 'bout loving and love, and wanting that one person close to you." He laughed then, still nervous, but something in his mind pleased him and he grunted, grinned even. "We're thinking 'bout our own young 'uns."

That was a scary enough idea that both boys

grunted and wiped their mouths in unconscious mimicry of English's nerves.

His next words almost knocked them over. "Might have already started one. Don't know yet, but it's certain possible."

Outside the barn, a commotion and the high pitch of Ruthie's voice caught the attention of the three and they got up quickly to go outside, away from the words and the forced closeness. Each of them had a lot to think about.

Jonas shook his head. "Hell, Tad, this is tough. I can't think on Ma as a woman!"

Burn went out into daylight, exposed and scared. He was getting married soon. Ruthie yelled at him, and he was laughing finally as he came to her rescue. She'd been trying to unharness the parson's horse and had gotten a few of the straps undone wrong, leaving bits and pieces hanging off a very nervous gelding.

Burn steadied the horse with a few pats on the neck, quietly explaining to the listening animal what was about to happen and why Ruthie had gotten her buckles wrong. Next he directed Ruthie on how to unhitch the animal correctly— a lesson the child needed to learn. He spent so much time going over the horse that the animal turned around to bite him just as Ruthie tugged on his arm to tell him that there were folks driving up.

"What folks?" he asked. In response, she turned

him around. He witnessed the arrival of several buggies carrying families with fathers driving, mamas cradling small children. And horses with *vaqueros* from the Carpenter ranch. No sign of the widow, which let Burn sigh in relief. But he recognized Arcy and the paint he had started maybe five years ago. Just behind him came Rogelio at the reins of a steady team, a woman beside him, three growing sons in the back. From the other direction, the doctor from Mancos was pulling up in his motorcar. Surprisingly this time the horses barely bothered to turn and look at the metal and rubber that moved on its own.

Burn slapped the horse lightly on the shoulder, then tied it to a post. He told Ruthie to throw down some good hay to keep the horse quiet. Before leaving her, he promised her that, come summer, he would teach her how to swim in Salt Valley pond where they had first become friends. That brought a big smile to her shining face.

And then his wife-to-be stepped out of the cabin and stood on the porch. Her hair was shiny and pinned up, she wore a new printed dress, so low in front that Burn blushed. It was fitted to her waist, then swept into a loose-flowing skirt, tight boots laced above her ankles. Lord, she was a pretty sight.

Maggie laughed at the sight of him. He was a mess—hay and horsehair everywhere, slobber on his shirt, but his face was cleanly shaven, and his pants and boots had been wiped, even polished. He wasn't any knight in shining armor as she'd heard of in stories, but he was hers, about to make that promise in front of a lot of folks. And she loved him.

Burn went toward her, up the few steps to the house to stand close but not touching. Not yet. She took a deep breath and watched his eyes shift to her bosom, and she smiled then, wanting so badly to touch him. His scent, of horses and a light sweat, dirt on his hands, was enough to make her almost dizzy. She directed him into the house, where a clean shirt was waiting on the wood chair where he'd sat so long with a dying old man. There was no sadness in the memory, only a sweet reminder of how they'd come to meet.

Burn did as he was told, passing by the parson who was eating. After drawing the curtain closed around the bed, he found the fresh white shirt and his fingers looked dark and clumsy against the fine material as he picked it up. Soft, each stitch made carefully. Her hands had worked these bits of thread to make his wedding shirt. Burn shivered as he changed out of his old shirt. He ran his fingers through his hair, and said dammit as he looked at his own refection in the tin mirror propped on the windowsill. It was then that he heard Maggie and their guests entering the cabin. When he was ready, he pulled back the curtain.

The preacher rose awkwardly and pulled on his coat. When Burn walked up to him, the man said: "Do you have any questions, son," he asked, "about the state of marriage?"

Son, huh? The man was younger than Burn by a good ten years. "No, sir, parson. I got me a damned . . . a good idea 'bout marriage and what happens next." Guess he had been direct enough since the parson blushed and went silent.

Burn walked to Maggie, and then was standing next to her. The parson got to talking at some length until the gathering became impatient. The parson, his name was Elijah Goodwin, finally got the idea and found his way to the heart of the ceremony.

When he finally asked Burn if he took "this woman to be his wife," Burn said his "I do" before the man was halfway through the question. At that all the men in the gathering laughed before their wives hushed them. At the last words, the witnesses cheered. The sound of a guitar, a singer telling a tale of marriage in high-note Spanish came next.

Maggie stepped in close to her man, her legal husband, and spoke gently into his ear. As she knew it would, the sound of Maggie English startled him. Then he, too, laughed, and in front of friends and neighbors, a few strangers, he kissed her as if they were alone in their own bed.

EPILOGUE

In early March, Burn started his day as he usually did, with a kiss to Maggie and a trip to the barn to feed out hay and check on the horses. Ruthie's roan Appaloosa was showing his age and Burn figured the girl was wanting something fancier, given all her hints about Beauty, but he wasn't ready to give up the mare yet.

Beauty didn't nicker at him first thing as he walked into the barn, but that old roan, he talked and fussed and even kicked at the stall boards. Burn went to the mare and froze in shock.

Next to the mare's belly, a small tail twisting with pleasure, was a buckskin filly nursing. And he'd missed the signs—the growing belly, that change to the muscles on the hindquarters, even the teats growing full, bagging up. Beauty had managed to find herself a suitor, back down near Springerville, and had herself a fine baby. The filly sure wasn't from the old stallion. He'd never throw that color out of a bay mare.

He'd been wondering all winter how they were going to live the next thirty years or so. Scrabbling for food on the dry land was one thing, making a comfortable life together was different. And he wasn't any cowpuncher, had

had to say no to the Widow Carpenter when she asked him to come work the old man's ranch.

And those automobiles, they were more and more what people wanted, not good horses, just tin and iron and tires that rolled. There wasn't much left for a mustanger. It'd kept him up nights, worrying on how he would take care of his family. Maggie thought she was expecting, too, maybe in the fall, if she was. Their life had to change.

The boys had come home for Christmas. Jonas had been the one to put the idea in his mind. The boy was working on those automobiles and had overheard two men talking about a game called polo, played on horseback. The Army up in Fort Robinson and folks around Rayado and Miami in New Mexico, they were chasing a ball and swinging long sticks and they needed good horses to play the game.

Staring at the buckskin filly nursing on her ma, it came to Burn that he could start all over again. He knew of a good stallion that Rogelio owned, and now he had two mares that could be bred. It would take a while, but the English name might have a chance, with these folks playing their polo and wanting as many good horses as a man like Burn English could train.

ABOUT THE AUTHOR

William A. Luckey was born in Providence, Rhode Island, but later went West to work with horses. "I've spent the past forty years dealing with rogue horses using my own methods to retrain and make them useful—I've evented, shown dressage, fox-hunted for twenty seasons, worked cattle, gone on five-day trail rides. I've owned over 150 horses personally, going back to when I was seven. I've actually been riding now for almost sixty years, and have taught riding for over forty years." *High Line Rider* appeared in 1985, the first of eleven Western novels published to date.

Center Point Large Print
600 Brooks Road / PO Box 1
Thorndike ME 04986-0001 USA

(207) 568-3717

US & Canada:
1 800 929-9108
www.centerpointlargeprint.com